CAPER

CAPER

PARNELL HALL

PEGASUS BOOKS
NEW YORK

CAPER

Pegasus Books LLC
80 Broad Street, 5th Floor
New York, NY 10004

Copyright © 2010 by Parnell Hall

First Pegasus Books cloth edition 2010

Interior design by Maria Fernandez

ISBN: 978-1-60598-104-8

10 9 8 7 8 6 5 4 3 2 1

Printed in the United States of America
Distributed by W. W. Norton & Company, Inc.

To Jim and Franny

1

I NEEDED TO HAVE FUN.

I'd just come off a bad case. I'd gotten involved with a hitman, nearly gotten shot. If you've never had the pleasure, trust me, it's overrated. Particularly if you're not accustomed to such things. I have a photo ID, but that's where any resemblance between me and a private investigator stops. I don't have car chases or fist fights or any of that stuff. I don't even carry a gun.

I work for a negligence lawyer, the type who advertises on TV: "Free consultation. No fee unless recovery. We will come to your home."

He won't of course. He'll send me. And I'll sit you down and get you to sign a retainer, and then I'll investigate your accident, which I could do in my sleep, they're all the same, hell, *I* could tell *you* what happened: you tripped on a crack in the sidewalk and broke your leg and you want to sue the City of New York.

It's dull as dishwater, and not the least bit dangerous. True, the clients tend to live in slums and crack houses, but I've actually never had a problem. The scary-looking dudes who make me nervous always assume I'm a cop, and give me a wide berth.

It's not like being shot.

Knock on wood.

But it isn't fun.

Far from it.

It's just a stopgap job in between my acting and writing gigs.

I've been doing it for years.

At any rate, having had a near-death experience I was up for anything. I was growing old, closing in on that final frontier, wondering was there one more adventure in my life before I shuffle off this mortal coil? Or something to that effect. I can't even get the quotes right anymore. Not that I ever could. Oh, imperfect, flawed, failure.

And so I spiraled down into a depressing abyss of despair and doldrums and decay.

I was ripe for adventure.

2

SHE CAME WAFTING INTO MY OFFICE LIKE A JOLT OF adolescence. I felt weak. I felt numb. Hormones were kicking in. Rockets were going off. Warning lights were flashing in my head. DANGER. TO YOUR BATTLE STATIONS. ALL SYSTEMS ON ALERT. THIS IS NOT A DRILL. YOU ARE A MARRIED MAN. REPEAT, YOU ARE A MARRIED MAN. NOT A DEPRESSED, PATHETIC GEEZER, LUSTING AFTER THE IMPOSSIBLE DREAM. LOOK IN THE MIRROR. REPEAT. LOOK IN THE MIRROR. IF THE MAN LOOKING BACK AT YOU IS NOT THE TWENTY-YEAR-OLD THAT YOU ENVISION YOURSELF TO BE, PUT YOUR LIBIDO DOWN AND STEP AWAY FROM THE HOT CHICK.

Did I mention I'm horny as hell? Well, keep it in mind.

Not that that's unusual. I'm a guy. Horny as hell is my default position. Has been ever since I was a teenager. Will be till the day I die. Only lately it's seemed more intense.

Maybe I'm just having a mid-life crisis. Maybe it's just the older we get the more self-aware. It's not that I'm thinking about sex more often, though I probably am, but merely the fact that I am *aware* that I am thinking about it, that the subconscious has become conscious, that I am now *thinking* about what I am thinking, which is the sort of stuff that therapists' dreams are made of. If I earned more money I could buy some analyst a condo.

For instance, when I see a woman I notice her breasts. That's nothing new. Mother Nature stuck them right there up front, hard to miss, and I am appreciative. Only discreetly so. I do not ogle, goggle, stare, wolf-whistle, rubberneck, or any other boorish behavior of the knuckle-dragging neanderthal type.

I don't.

Only women *think* I do.

At least, that's the impression I get. When an attractive woman comes walking toward me, I am convinced that *she* thinks I'm looking at her breasts. Because she gives me that impression. *She* looks at her breasts. As if to say, "My God, why is he staring? Is my bra unhooked? Is my nipple exposed? Did I forget to wear a shirt? Why is that disgusting pervert looking at me?"

I realize this is all in my head, that is not what is happening at all, what I am observing is simple eye avoidance. The woman looks down, shifts her eyes away from those of the stranger. I know that plain as day.

Doesn't help.

As far as I'm concerned, she looked at her breasts because I'm a disgusting pig.

And to a certain extent I'm right. Because, whether or not *she's* thinking about her breasts at that point, *I* am. So for all practical purposes I've become that boorish lout that I believe she perceives me to be.

But I digress.

I was talking about my client.

Jennifer Weldon couldn't have been more than twenty-two or twenty-three, most likely younger. She had blonde hair, lopped off and curling in, a pear-shaped halo around her head. Blue eyes, turned-up nose, pouty mouth, chirpy cheerleader look. That's probably more description than I've ever given a client of mine. Of course, she was wearing a scoop-neck pullover. I guess I just wanted to show I was looking at her face.

I smiled hello.

She looked at her breasts.

I offered her a chair, sat behind my desk. Grabbed a pen and a legal pad, flipped open to a random page. It's a good tactic, puts clients at their ease. I've done it several times. I don't think I've ever written a note.

"What can I do for you?" I said.

"It's my daughter."

I reevaluated my assessment. This woman had a child? What, did she get knocked up when she was fifteen? Kid must be one or two. Guy must have skipped town. She must want me to find him. What a sordid affair.

"You have a daughter?"

"Of course I have a daughter. That's why I need help." She sucked in her breath. "David doesn't know I'm here."

"David?"

"My husband."

"You have a husband?"

She looked at me as if I were a moron. "Yes, I've got a husband. And he doesn't know I'm here."

"I don't understand."

"Of course you don't. I haven't told you yet." She sighed. "I'm not telling this well. I guess I'm upset."

"What's the matter?"

"It's my daughter. She's headstrong. I can't deal with her."

"How old is your daughter?"

5

"Sixteen."

I blinked. "You have a teenage daughter?"

"Yes."

"You're not old enough to have a teenage daughter."

She scowled. "Are you flirting with me? I find that highly inappropriate."

"I'm not flirting with you. I'm having age issues. It has nothing to do with your case. You got a teenage daughter you can't deal with. What's the problem with her?"

"She's skipping school."

I smiled, shook my head. "I'm not a truant officer."

"No, of course not. But . . ."

"But what?"

"You're an investigator. You could find out."

"Find out what?"

"Find out why."

"She probably doesn't like it."

"Yes, that's very clever. Can you do it?"

"I don't know what you want me to do. You want me to find your daughter?"

"Heavens, no."

"You *don't* want me to find your daughter?

"I don't *need* you to find my daughter. She's in school. At least, I hope she is."

"She's not a runaway?"

"Certainly not. She lives with us."

"Where?"

"In our apartment."

"Where's that?"

"Park Avenue and Eighty-fourth."

"Nice address. I may have to adjust my fee."

"I'm glad you think this is funny."

"I don't think it's funny. I'm just trying to understand the situation. Which is a little difficult, because you haven't painted a very clear picture. You want me to drag this out of you in a way you obviously find irritating, or would you like to take a deep breath and just lay it on me?"

She actually took a deep breath.

I kept my eyes on her face.

"Sharon's a bright girl, does well, never gave us any trouble, gets her homework in on time, gets good grades. Comes home on time. Doesn't hang out with the wrong crowd."

"The wrong crowd?"

She cocked her head. "Oh, my God. You're being condescending? Judgmental?"

"Not at all."

"Really? I could practically hear a disapproving 'tut tut.'"

"Have you had these auditory hallucinations often?"

"Stop trying to be clever. You're no good at it."

"I know. Only one of my many failings. I don't suppose you'll be hiring me then."

"You don't want the job?"

I didn't. My client had gone from being a red-hot mama to an overprotective mama. One immune to my wit. She also reminded me too forcibly of the high-powered young women executive types who scared the shit out of me when I was fresh out of college working job-jobs, making the rounds, and trying to get my sea legs.

"I don't know what you want me to do. You tell me your daughter's skipping school. I ask you where she is, you tell me she's *in* school. She's a bright girl, gets good grades, doesn't hang around with the wrong crowd. Your story doesn't add up. Either there's something you're not telling me, or I don't know why you're here."

She stared at me defiantly for a moment, then dissolved into tears.

Oh, dear.

Attractive weeping women are not my forte. Should I put my arm around her? Pat her on the shoulder? Look down her shirt?

I took her in my arms, averted my eyes, let her cry herself out. She pulled away, snuffled, fumbled in her purse for a tissue.

"All right," I said. "What's the story.

She snuffled again, looked up, set her chin.

"I think she's turning tricks."

3

RICHARD ROSENBERG COULD NOT HAVE LOOKED MORE SKEPTICAL had I told him I was going to Mars. "Why did she hire you?"

"She's afraid her daughter's turning tricks."

"I got all that. Why you?"

"I'm a private detective."

"In the loosest sense of the word. Stanley, this is the first question to consider every time you have a potential client. Why are they hiring you? I mean you, specifically. Why would any reasonably intelligent, rational person, who had not completely taken leave of their senses, ever think of hiring you?"

"*You* hired me."

"For the most menial job possible. A trained chimpanzee could do the work you do. Assuming he could drive a car."

"That's rather sexist."

"What?"

"Assuming the chimpanzee's male. Or do you only hire male chimpanzees?"

"It's no laughing matter, Stanley. This is what always happens to you. You walk into something, wide-eyed, innocent, naive, trusting. Next thing you know you're wanting me to bail you out of jail."

"When have you ever bailed me out of jail?"

"When have I not? Granted, I've never put up any money, but I've got you released on your own recognizance. The point is, you're a credulous fool. What do you really know about this woman?"

"She's pretty."

"Ah. Then vetting her is unnecessary. A pretty woman couldn't be up to anything."

"She paid me cash."

"Cash is good. I happen to like cash. But *why* did she pay you in cash?"

"She didn't want her husband to find out."

"Why not?"

"She thought it would upset him."

"And you bought that?"

"Why not? It *would* upset him."

"More than it upset her? Stanley, you have this romantic idea about parents and children. You think no girl with a father can be a hooker. Trust me, they all have them."

"These are nice people."

"All your clients are nice people. Including the prostitutes, drug addicts, scam artists, and hitmen. They're all really nice. The fact that they lead you into temptation is entirely coincidental and not to be inferred."

"Are you telling me not to take the case?"

"You took the money, didn't you?"

"Yes."

"Then you took the case. The only question now is how badly you handle it."

"You have any advice on that?"

"Yes."

"What?"

"Don't fuck it up."

"That's your only opinion?"

"No, but it's the best advice I can give you. That's what you're here for, isn't it? You don't want permission. You've already taken the case. You don't want my blessing, because you know you'll never get it. You just want my advice."

"I just wanted to tell you I may have to alter my schedule. It seemed only fair to do so, since you happen to be one of those people you disdain. You know, those who hire me."

"Oh, we're back to chimpanzees again. Speaking of which, have you turned in your cases? I could use a good laugh."

"A good laugh?"

"Well, most of you cases *are* pathetic."

"They're *your* cases."

"Not until I take them. They're *potential* cases. If they look good, I file suit. If they don't, I have a form rejection letter. Would you like to know what percentage of cases you handle get that letter?"

"Is it higher than average?"

"That would be hard. The percentage of cases I take is actually rather small. True, I file more cases than any other attorney in New York. But I investigate a hell of a lot more. At least, you do."

"Sounds like I should be making more money."

"You don't pay chimpanzees. You give 'em bananas."

"Great. Can you find another chimpanzee to pinch-hit while I save a young girl from a life of sin?"

Richard shook his head, pityingly. "God, you mix metaphors."

4

SERGEANT MACAULLIF DIDN'T CALL ME A MORON. WHICH made me nervous, because he always does. Whether I've taken a case, finished a case, asked him to trace somebody, brought him a piece of evidence, or merely said, "Good morning," his response has always been the same. "You're a moron." In the event I've displayed more than usual ineptitude, and sometimes even if I haven't, his response is, "You're a fucking moron." Which is ironically less and less true as the years go on.

This time he just nodded and said, "She pay cash?"

"Yes."

"Way to go."

"You think this is a good idea?"

"Taking cash is the best idea ever. I suppose technically I should turn you in to the IRS, but, hey, if you don't declare it, there's really nothing I can do."

"MacAullif."

"What?"

"You don't think I'm doing the wrong thing."

MacAullif leaned back in his desk chair, a somewhat precarious position lately. Always a beefy cop, the sergeant had put on weight, would be needing to let the waist of his trousers out again soon. He twiddled his thumbs. "You have any milestone birthdays coming up?"

"Why?"

"It's kind of like a stripper-gram for private eyes. A teenage-hooker-gram."

"MacAullif."

"I'm not saying you have sex with her. It's better than that. You find her, you talk to her, you straighten her out. You feel great about yourself. You're the white knight on the steed, saving the maiden in distress. Which is the role you always cast yourself in. I would say whoever set this up probably brought it in for less than a grand. Including the money they paid you. Which is like a bonus. You get paid for feeling good. How much did they give you?"

"Two hundred dollars."

"What's that supposed to buy?"

"One day's work."

"That's today?"

"Starting tomorrow."

"Call it a day an a half. Actually, two. Today's shot for you. Considering the time you're wasting telling everyone. I assume you've already told Rosenberg."

"He's my boss."

"I'm sure he's proud. You don't suppose *he* set this up, did he? As a sort of bonus?"

"Richard?"

"Right, right, it's Rosenberg. He doesn't know the word bonus. Just the word contingency. Which you don't share in, do you?

Richard gets thirty-three and a third percent. You get five bucks an hour and two cents a mile."

"It's a little more than that."

"I'm glad to hear it. You maintaining a New York apartment, and all."

"Any time you're through screwing around."

"Huh? Oh, you want something? What could that possibly be? You need me to find this hooker? Surely Mommy took care of that."

"I'd like to know I'm not doing anything wrong."

MacAullif rolled his eyes. "Oh, my god, what a straight line. I don't know what to say, it's too damn easy. You always do something wrong. Given a fifty-fifty chance, you'll pick wrong every time."

"All right, then. How about illegal."

MacAullif shook his head despairingly. "Moron."

"What?"

"Prostitution *is* illegal. It's illegal to begin with. Unless you're making a citizen's arrest and dragging this girl down to the station. You are compounding a felony and conspiring to conceal a crime."

"That's the wrong answer."

"Yeah, but it's the one you expected to hear."

It was, actually. When I get going on a fantasy, there's nothing to bring me back to reality like a good, hard, slap in the face from MacAullif.

"Would you say that any private eye hired to bring back a teenage runaway was conspiring to conceal a crime?"

"Is this girl a runaway?"

"No."

"She's living at home?"

"Yes."

"What do they need you for? Why don't they give her a good talking to, ground her, and get on with their lives?"

"She doesn't want her husband to know."

"A teenage hooker has a husband?"

"Her mother."

"Oh. And what's the mother like?"

"Oh."

"Good God, you're let another attractive woman wrap you around her finger. What was the mother like? What a stupid question. I'm assuming she's got tits and ass and a pulse."

"She is rather attractive."

"No kidding. Otherwise you'd never let yourself get talked into this for no money."

"She paid cash."

"Two hundred bucks. Her analyst makes that in an hour. A fifty-minute hour."

"What are you trying to say?"

"I'm not trying to say anything. I'm just wondering how long I have to keep talking before you realize this is not a good investment."

"That's what I said in the first place."

"Not in those terms. You never ask anything simply and directly. You bring up the whole thing as if it were a wonderful opportunity, waiting for me to shoot you down."

"Are you shooting me down?"

"Do you see me applauding? I can give you enough reasons not to take the case. I assume it's a moot point, because the money's in your pocket. You've already taken it, all you want now is validation. Which you're not going to get. Which you probably knew before you came in the door. A less astute observer might wonder why you came."

"You don't?"

"Don't be silly. I know exactly why you came."

"Why is that?"

"You don't want to go home."

5

AT THE ART OF MORTAL CONVERSATION, ALICE HAS NO equal. I no longer compete. Not that it does any good. Alice can pick up on my lack of response, turn my unwillingness to engage into a vile, reprehensible, passive-aggressive action, the likes of which have never appeared in the annals of marital discord.

Bad as that is, any response is worse. Alice is a master of sarcasm and irony, the subtle, understated, deadpan zinger, couched like a time bomb within the most innocuous phrase.

Worse, she is unpredictable. It is totally impossible to brace oneself against Alice, because her responses run the gamut. She can decimate me with a simple "That's nice," a throw-away murmur while leaving the room, a thin smile on her lips, a twinkle in her eyes. And I know, I just know, I've been utterly stupid.

But of all the tactics in Alice's arsenal, by far the most devastating is her understanding-and-supportive mode.

"Don't worry, Stanley, we'll get you out of it."

"There's nothing to get out of. It's just a job."

"I know, and it's nice of you to take on the extra work. But, trust me, we'll get by."

"It's not a question of getting by. It's a question of helping the girl."

"And she's an escort?"

I'd called her an escort to avoid using the term teenage hooker. That seemed unnecessarily incendiary. I chucked out whore and streetwalker for similar reasons. Strumpet, harlot, and lady of the evening were too archaic. It came down to call girl or escort. Escort won out for not including the word girl.

"Yes."

"She works for a service?"

"I didn't say she works for a service."

"Then how does she meet her clientele?"

"I have no idea."

"Don't be silly. If she's a paid escort, she works for someone."

"Well, I don't know."

"Her mother didn't either?"

"No."

"And yet she knows she works for a service. I wonder how she found out."

I said nothing, waited for Alice to drop the subject.

As if.

"I mean, if she found an ad, or a business card, or a telephone number, that would be a dead giveaway. She wouldn't send you out in the dark. So, how'd the mother know it was an escort service?"

"The mother *didn't* know it was an escort service."

"So you don't know it's an escort service?"

"I guess I don't."

"Then why call it an escort service?"

"I don't know."

"I mean, you can't expect to make much progress if you're that haphazard with your work. You wind up spending a week looking for a nonexistent escort service."

"That *would* be silly."

"No kidding. How old is this daughter?"

"Oh."

"Oh? That's a very bad sign. Is it possible the mother didn't mention the age of the daughter?"

"She's sixteen."

"Stanley."

"Which is why she needs saving."

"From what? She doesn't work for any service. They don't hire sixteen-year-old girls. Not if they want to stay in business."

"Maybe the word escort is a little strong. Maybe this is just something the girl is doing for some friends."

"And you're shooting yourself in the head because when you were sixteen you didn't know girls like that."

"Times were different then. Man had just discovered fire."

"Don't give me the geezer bit. You're not that old."

Alice pushed back from the computer. That didn't mean she was finished using it. A champion multitasker, my wife is perfectly capable of blogging or tweeting, or whatever those online people do these days, without missing a beat in her interrogation. "All right, let's get down to the heart of the matter. You've been hired to save a young girl from a fate worse than death. You're utterly embarrassed, and you don't want to talk about it. I find that very cute. How are you supposed to contact this girl? Tell me you're not soliciting sex from her."

"That would be entrapment."

Her mouth fell open. "Entrapment? That's your only objection?"

"Just because the subject is distasteful doesn't mean the work shouldn't be done."

"I know. You can justify anything. Hell, you worked for a hitman."

"If you don't want me to take the case . . ."

"I didn't say that."

"I can always turn it down."

"How are you supposed to recognize this girl."

"Oh."

Alice's eyes widened. "You have her picture?" She held out her hand. "Give."

I took out my wallet, passed the snapshot over. I did so reluctantly. Sharon looked good: fresh, clean, virginal, young. But she didn't look sixteen. Closer to ten.

Alice looked at the picture, shook her head disparagingly, as if I were to blame for the girl's downfall. "Oh, my God. She's just a child."

"Yes."

"It's disgusting. Degrading. Awful."

"It's sleazy as hell. I feel dirty just thinking about it. You want me to get out?"

Alice looked at me as if I were a moron.

"Are you kidding? You've gotta help her."

6

I PICKED SHARON UP AT THREE FORTY-FIVE AT P.S. 64. POOR choice of words, when dealing with a teenage hooker. I didn't pick her up. I got on her tail. Another poor choice of words.

This was not good. I hadn't even begun the case, and already queasy overtones of pedophilia were making me want to lose my lunch. It didn't help that she looked about ten, which I sort of expected, since her mother looked like a teenager. At least I didn't look at her breasts. She didn't have any. Though it occurred to me I must have looked in order to ascertain that. Anyway, she came bopping out of school at three forty-five, the same fresh face as in the picture, and the body of a kid. Cotton pullover shirt, ribbon in her hair. Was she wearing bobby sox? Why did I think of that? What the hell were bobby sox, anyway? I mean, you think of Annette Funicello and Frankie Avalon. Maybe I was thinking of the song, "When a girl changes from bobby sox to stockings." Now why did I think of that? Did Frankie sing it? Good Lord, what an inappropriately appropriate song.

It occurred to me she didn't look like a hooker, but maybe that's what men want. A hooker who looks like a little girl.

Okay, this is the point where I step in, scare the shit out of her, send her home. *Scared Straight*. A documentary way back when. Notable for using words you couldn't say on television that got by because it was such a good cause. Peter Falk took kids at risk, showed them what life would be like for them in prison, huge tattooed convicts fucking them up the ass and trading them for smokes. Kids were all out of trouble when the show aired, indicating the lesson worked, though I seem to recall the tabloids taking great delight in reporting any subsequent arrests.

At any rate, if that was the role I had to play, so be it. At this point it wasn't the money. There she was, a sweet young thing, and nobody, but nobody, was getting their hands on her.

I no sooner had that thought when a car pulled up to the curb, honked, and she ran over and hopped into the front seat.

With her bookbag. The bookbag killed me. Despite the fact she'd just come out of school, it looked like a prop.

The car pulled away from the curb.

I hadn't seen the driver. Not that the car had tinted windows, just that the passenger side was to the curb, and the car was at an angle so that I couldn't see in when she opened the door.

Well, that was just great. Not only had I failed to save the girl from a life of sin, but she had managed to accomplish it right under my very nose.

I rushed out into the street and hailed a cab. Fat chance. There were no taxis anywhere. Just school buses clogging the street. Except for one small fissure the girl's car had managed to squeeze through. I hadn't caught the plate, or even the make of the car.

I ran around the buses, spotted the car at a red light at the end of the block. What the hell kind of car was it? It looked new, it looked expensive, it looked like its occupant and I didn't belong in the same league.

Then, miracle of miracles, a taxi squeezed by the bus, its light like a beacon of hope. I hailed it, hopped in.

The driver, one Felipe Rodriguez, according to the license posted on the glove compartment, said, "Where to?"

"Follow that car," I told him.

I expected him to argue. He just said, "The Lexus?"

So that's what it was. "Yeah, the Lexus. Can you catch it?"

"Are you kiddin' me?"

The cabby popped the clutch. At least he would have if there had been a clutch. The cab, of course, was an automatic. I wondered when was the last time a cabby actually popped a clutch. Then my neck snapped like a rubber band and the cab rocketed down the street. Within seconds we were right on the Lexus's tail.

"Hey, don't let him know we're following."

"Why should he? This is how I always drive."

I shut up, checked my vertebrae for whiplash. My spinal cord seemed intact.

The mad cabbie tailed the Lexus to Fifth Avenue and 88th. Where, to my delight, it slowed, signaled, and . . .

Drove into an underground garage.

"Shit."

"Too bad," the cabbie said.

"Can you park?"

"Huh?"

"Pull in and park. I'll pay the fee."

"It's a private garage."

I knew that. I asked the question with no hope, the way you will sometimes, even though you know the answer.

I paid off the cab and got out. Weighed my options. I had the license plate number. I could trace the car. But that wasn't going to help me now.

I went around to the front. It was your typical Fifth Avenue building, brass and glass door, with artistic bric-a-brac. I pushed it open, went inside.

There was a liveried doorman at a desk. "May I help you?" he said, in a neutral tone, neither encouraging nor disapproving, ready to go in either way should I turn out to be a bill collector or a wealthy tenant's brother.

I gave him my warmest smile. "I think a friend of mine just pulled into the garage."

"Oh?"

"Yes. But I'm not sure. Do you have a video monitor?"

"Yes."

"Does it cover the garage?"

The doorman had a cultivated supercilious arrogance that did not bode well. "Who's your friend?"

"I'd rather not say, in case I'm wrong."

"I see."

"So whose car is it?"

He smiled. "I'd rather not say in case you're wrong."

I went outside, flipped open my cell phone, called MacAullif. "Can you trace a license plate number for me?"

"Whose is it?"

"One of the hooker's johns. Can you do it, MacAullif? It would really help."

"Why? What the fuck are you doing? You trying to rescue this girl, or take down her johns?"

"Come on, MacAullif. The guy picked her up in his car, took her to his Fifth Avenue apartment. Got an underground garage, doesn't even have to take her by the front desk. He's got her up there now doing God knows what."

"So?"

"I'd like to know where she is."

"Why?"

"Huh?"

"What's your plan? You gonna bust in on 'em, drag her outta there? How you gonna get past the front desk?"

"She's sixteen."

"So what?"

"It's a crime. A crime is being committed."

"So."

"You can go in to stop a crime. Even without a warrant."

"You're not a cop."

"Anyone can make a citizen's arrest."

"Right. You go to the front desk, say, 'Hi. I think one of your tenants is banging a teenage hooker. I don't have a warrant and I'm not a cop, but I'd like to go up and see.'"

"I get the point."

"Of course you do, you fucking, annoying, scumbag son of a bitch. You knew it before you made the call. You don't want to go in. You want me to send the vice squad to made the bust, and a SWAT team to kick down the door. On the flimsiest, thirdhand, hearsay evidence ever."

"I saw him with my own eyes."

"Really? What does he look like?"

"Well, I saw his car."

"Oh, my god. You're a moron of the highest order. Look, I'll trace the license number for you, but I won't drop the two homicides I'm working on to do it. I'll have it for you by tomorrow. If that doesn't allow you to change into your Superman suit and save the day, I'm sorry, but I happen to have this job. Jesus Christ, what did I ever do to deserve this," MacAullif said, and hung up the phone.

7

SHE WAS OUT AT A QUARTER TO SIX. NEARLY TWO HOURS. I
hope he paid her well. She didn't look the worse for wear, but then,
she was young. Give her a couple of years and it would take its toll.

Not if I had anything to say about it.

I stepped out in the middle of the sidewalk, blocked her way.
"Hi, there."

She didn't react like a hooker. Unless she pegged me for a cop.
She sure didn't act like I was a john. She drew back, and her face
contorted into an *ooh-gross!* expression. "Who are you?"

"The real question is who are you?"

"What?"

"You're at a crossroads, sweetheart. And you don't wanna take
the wrong turn."

"What are you talking about?"

"You know damn well what I'm talking about. You may think
it's easy money, but it's not. It's the hardest money you ever made."

"You're crazy."

"I know you think so now. In a couple of years you'll think different."

"Who are you?"

"I'm your best friend. I wanna help you."

"If you don't go away I'll scream."

"That wouldn't be a good idea."

"Why not?"

"Cops will come. You don't want that."

"*You* don't want that. Old man, bothering a girl."

"As opposed to the ones who give you money."

"You want to give me money?"

"Absolutely not."

"Wait'll I tell the cops you offered me money."

"I *didn't* offer you money."

"*I* say you did. Let's see who they believe."

And, just like that, she went from teenage nymphet to hardened whore. I could see her ratting me out to the cops, playing it virginal, laughing up her sleeve.

"Look, Sharon."

Her eyes widened. "You know my name. How do you know my name?"

"I'm your guardian angel."

"You're a lunatic. You keep away from me."

"How much did the guy in the Lexus pay you?"

Her mouth fell open, and her eyes bugged out of her head. "What?!"

"I know what you did. I'm just wondering what it was worth. In money, I mean. Not from a moral point of view."

Her lip trembled. "Leave me alone."

"Fine. I'll leave you alone. Just think on this. It's two A.M., you can't sleep, you haven't eaten in days, haven't showered in weeks. But you need a fix, so you pull some loser off the street, some strung-out freak who isn't afraid of AIDS because he's probably got it himself, and you offer every single orifice in the hope the loser actually has some cash. And it's a toss-up, a fifty-fifty chance, whether the creep will slip you a couple of bucks or simply slit your throat. And you don't really care much which. How does that sound?"

She stared at me a moment. Then she burst out crying, and ran off down the street.

8

"YOU IDIOT!"

Sharon's mother looked angry enough to hurl a paperweight. Thank god I don't have one. I sat behind my desk, prepared to brace myself in case Jennifer Weldon decided to come across it. "What's the matter?"

"You son of a bitch! My daughter came home in tears. She was accosted on the street by an insane man, spewing vile filth."

"She took it hard?"

"You admit it was you?"

"Of course it was me."

"What, are you nuts? Are you trying to traumatize the girl?"

"Yes, of course."

Jennifer blinked. "What?"

"I was doing *Scared Straight*. You know, with Peter Falk."

"What are you talking about?"

"Never mind, you're too young. I was putting the fear of God in the girl to leave the life of sin."

"Who asked you to do that?"

"Well, I had to do something. I only had one day."

"Did I ask you to *reform* my daughter? To *scare* my daughter? To even *talk* to my daughter? No. All I asked you to do was *follow* my daughter."

"I followed your daughter."

"That's *all* you were supposed to do. Follow her and report back to me. Was that so hard?"

"I don't see why you're so upset."

"You traumatized a young girl."

"Bullshit. This is New York City. Things like that happen all the time." I put up my hands. "I know, I know, I'm giving the city a bad rap. I like it here. Things like that don't happen all the time. But in a city this size, that's all I was saying. Trust me, she'll get over it."

"I'm glad you're so sure. She happened to be very upset."

"Did she tell you where she was when I spoke to her?"

"Yeah. On the street. In the middle of the goddamned street."

"Before that."

"Huh?"

"Did she tell you where she was before that? She got out of school, walked out in the street, and got picked up by the first car that slowed down."

"Yeah. Danny Goldstein. Got his driver's license. I shouldn't let her ride with him, but I do."

"What?"

"You don't approve? Pardon me but I'm not taking my parenting advice from you."

"Danny Goldstein has a Lexus?"

"It's his parents' car. Probably a Lexus. I don't know."

"You had me follow her when she was being picked up by a classmate?"

"He's not a classmate. He's a year older. Goes to Hunter."

"Good for him." I was having trouble controlling my temper. "Why did you have me follow her if you knew she was going home with a friend?"

"I didn't know she was going home with him. You think she tells me anything? So, you really screwed things up."

I took a breath. Tried to keep the steam from spewing out my ears. "Yes, I did. Without getting into whose fault it was, let's just say nothing was accomplished. No harm, no foul. Your daughter got scared by a random guy in the street. She'll get over it. So will I, and, believe it or not, so will you. Here's your money back. Find some other guy and start over."

That rocked her in her sockets. There's nothing like the shock of someone acting against their own best interests to grab your attention. For the first time since I met her, she lost some of her self assurance.

"You don't want the money?"

"I don't want the grief. You think I did a bad job, fine. Let's take a page out of Bob Dylan's book and pretend that we never met."

"Huh?"

"Oh, hell, you're too young for Dylan. This just ain't my day."

She was really agitated. I could tell because her chest was rising and falling inside a loose purple cotton top that tended to gape every time she leaned forward. No, I was not looking, I don't know where I got that image.

"Did I ask you for the money back? I didn't ask you for the money back. I paid you, you did the job. You may have done it poorly, but you did it, and I always pay my way. The job is over, finished, done. Give me your report and I'll get out of here."

"My report?"

"Yes."

"You expect a written report? I thought you didn't want your husband to know."

"Not a written report. A report. Tell me what you did."

"I told you what I did."

"You told me like an old woman. I want to hear it like a private eye."

I probably could have given her a better account of the grammatical misconstructions of those sentences than I could of my surveillance techniques, but the customer is always right. I whipped out my pocket notebook and flipped it open. This time it actually had notes in it.

I cleared my throat, dredged up recollections of private eye books and movies for the appropriate lingo. "I staked out P.S. 64 at three oh five. Subject emerged three forty-seven, stood on sidewalk. Three forty-nine, gray Lexus pulled up to the curb and subject hopped into the front seat. I followed the Lexus to the private underground garage of an apartment building on the corner of Fifth Avenue and Eighty-eighth Street."

I broke off at the look on her face. "What's the matter?"

"That isn't Danny Goldstein's address."

9

I WASN'T FIRED. DAMN IT. I HAVE TO TELL YOU, IT'S A HELL OF
a job when not getting fired is bad news.

I got Sexy Psycho Mom out of my office and called MacAullif.
"You trace that plate?"

"I'm getting to it."

"You gonna get to it soon?"

"You got an appointment with your client?"

"I had it."

"She fire you?"

"No such luck."

I gave MacAullif a rundown of my meeting with Mom. Need-
less to say, he was amused.

"So, you pulled a Peter Falk on the girl."

"You've seen it?"

"Of course, I've seen it. Bullshit, of course. Nothing scares these
hardass punks. Prison is like a merit badge. You ain't done hard
time, you're a wimp."

"Yeah, yeah, fine. Can you trace the fucking plate."

"Oooh! No one taught you to say please?"

"I got a short fuse on this one, MacAullif. I just got royally reamed for doing the right thing."

"That must be unusual for you. Doing the right thing, I mean. Getting bawled out is par for the course."

"I got your meaning. Can you trace the plate?"

"I will bump it up on my priority list. It was twenty-seventh. I can probably make it twelve. I get anything, I'll give you a call. You're working, aren't you? I mean for Rosenberg. You're not staking out the school all day."

No, I wasn't. I called the switchboard, told Wendy/Janet, Richard Rosenberg's twin switchboard girls, I was back on the clock. They're not twins, by the way, they don't look anything alike. They just have identical voices, so I can never tell which one I'm talking to.

Wendy/Janet was surprised to hear I was back on the job, largely because Richard had never mentioned I was off it, probably on the theory that if she beeped me with a case and I was close enough, I'd go.

I did three cases for Richard, all trip-and-falls, and was back in front of P.S. 64 by three fifteen.

Sharon came out at 3:45, laughing and chatting with a bunch of other girls, and walked down the street swinging her book bag just as if she were one of them, which, in a way, she was.

I followed the gaggle across town, losing girls on almost every corner, a nice metaphor for my life, actually, until finally I was down to one.

I watched her from across the street. She walked up into a newsstand in the middle of the block. I wondered if she was going to purchase cigarettes. If so, she was underage, and I could bust her for it. Wouldn't that be a hell of a thing. MacAullif would be proud. If he ever got done laughing.

No such luck. She came out sporting candy. A Milky Way. Bad for her teeth, no doubt. I could issue a stern warning, get my picture in *Oral Hygienists Monthly*. Or registered as a sex offender.

She flounced down the street, swinging her book bag and eating her candy. She looked like she might start skipping. If she did, I was really going to lose it. There's nothing in the private eye manual about skipping.

Three blocks later she turned onto Park Avenue. And, oh, the wonderful feeling, knowing I'm on the street where she lived.

I whipped out my cell phone, called MacAullif. "How's your homicide coming?"

"About how you'd expect. Some gangbanger dissed the wrong dealer, got shot for his trouble. All we gotta do is put the names to it."

"You make is sound easy."

"Piece of cake. We got an eyewitness."

"Oh?"

"Rival dealer wants to see the competition go down."

"Think he's telling the truth?"

"There's a damn good chance. There's also a chance *he's* the perp. And the other dealer will finger him."

"What do you do in that case?"

"Put 'em in a cage and let 'em fight it out."

"I'm glad you have no political aspirations."

"Why?"

"Rather racist statement."

"Oh? I don't recall mentioning the race of either dealer. You making assumptions about them? I would say that's rather racist."

I could imagine MacAullif grinning as he hung up the phone. The son of a bitch got me again. Hoist by my own liberal petard.

My cell phone rang.

It was MacAullif. "Why did you call me?"

"Huh?"

"You didn't call me to bullshit about my homicide. Why did you call me?"

"Oh."

"What's new with the case?'

"I followed the girl."

"And?"

"She went home."

"And?"

"Now she's home."

"You're waiting outside her apartment?"

"Yeah."

"You don't know when she's coming out?"

"No."

"You *did* call me just to bullshit."

"Well, it's boring."

"Get used to it," MacAullif said, and hung up the phone.

He called back ten minutes later. "I traced the plate."

"Oh?"

"Got a pencil?"

"I'm standing in the street."

"I'm sitting in my office. You got a pencil?"

"I gotta get it out."

I dug in my jacket pocket for a pad and pencil.

"You wanna know why I traced the plate?" MacAullif said.

"Because I asked you to."

"That was yesterday. I didn't trace it yesterday. You know why?"

"You were busy."

"I was busy yesterday. I'll be busy tomorrow. You know what's different about today?"

"You weren't busy?"

"I'm *always* busy. But today, you called me on the phone, you didn't bug me about the plate. I called you back, you didn't bug me

35

about the plate. See what happens? I start resenting you less, and I do you a favor."

"This must be really good."

"What?"

"What you got."

"Why do you say that?"

"The slow roll."

"Huh?"

"You're like a poker player with a winning hand. You know, who's torturing you with it, letting you think you've won, before flipping over the hole cards to dork you completely."

"It *is* rather good," MacAullif admitted.

"I knew it. Let's have it."

"The car is registered to a Jason Blake."

"Doesn't ring a bell."

"I didn't think it would. Forty-five years of age, married man, one kid. Lives at Five Twenty-one Fifth Avenue."

"That's the guy. What's the punch line?"

I could practically see MacAullif smile, the cat who swallowed the cream.

"He's a congressman."

10

After MacAullif's phone call, I was a little less bored. Sharon's john was a congressman. Granted, he was probably a one-night stand, unless Sharon satisfied some kinky, congressional urge I didn't want to know about, still it was an interesting tidbit.

I called Alice. "You on the computer?"

"Why?"

"I want you to Google someone."

"Is this for your case?"

"Yes."

"Please tell me it's not a high school girl."

"It isn't."

"Good, 'cause you get into Facebook and tweets and twitters, and you don't wanna go there."

"I don't?"

"You can't pick up your e-mail without help. I'm not guiding you around the Net."

"Hey, I can Google. I'm just not at a computer."

"Nerds in India thank you."

"India?"

"Haven't you ever called for tech support?"

"I always ask you."

"Who do you want Googled?"

"A congressman."

"What district?"

"How the hell should I know? I assume in New York City. He lives in New York City."

"Got an address?"

"Actually, I do."

"That would narrow it down somewhat. Give me what you got."

Alice typed the information into the computer. Not necessarily in Google. Alice has search engines the general public has only heard rumors of.

"Oooh!" Alice said.

"What?"

"This is not just any congressman. He's the driving force behind Proposition Nineteen."

"What's that?"

"A bill to raise the age of consent in New York."

"Raise it?"

"Yeah. Right now it's eighteen. Anyone under eighteen is a minor. You have sex with them, it's statutory rape. He wants to raise it to nineteen. Anyone under nineteen's a minor. So he's the All-American boy for God, family, and Mom's apple pie. That's your pervert?"

"That's the guy."

"You following him tonight?"

"I hope not."

"Huh?"

"I don't want him anywhere near this girl."

"Stanley."

"Don't Stanley me. I'm not going to stand by and let it happen."

"You can't stop it. You have no authority. Even if you did, don't you have to have grounds?"

"I've got grounds."

"Legal grounds. That would satisfy a judge."

"I'm not a cop. I'm not getting a warrant."

"What are you doing?"

"I have no idea."

"Stanley."

"That's her! Gotta go!"

I snapped the cell phone closed and set off in pursuit of the nymphet, who was hightailing it down the street with the purposeful stride of a young lady up for action. I was not up for action. I was up for hanging around outside her apartment bitching about the fact that I had nothing to do. That sure beat the hell out of rousting some john the girl happened to pick up, pissing her off again, and alerting her to the fact that my accosting her in the street was not just an accidental, one-time encounter.

I don't mind walking fast, I prefer it to dawdling. Still, there is an upper limit, a comfort zone, beyond which it becomes a major pain in the ass, and I was puffing heavily as the girl turned east on 86th. I could have used a rest. Instead I tried to shorten the distance. If the girl was going to pick someone up, the wide, commercial cross street seemed the place to do it.

She didn't, however. If anything, she quickened her pace. She crossed Lexington, kept going east to Third Avenue, caught a break in the traffic, and crossed 86th Street, heading uptown. I did not catch a break in the traffic, and nearly got killed trying to follow, which probably would have got me a mention in the *New York Post*. Somehow I made it with no worse consequences than several irate car horns and an occasional finger.

I hit the sidewalk just in time to see Sharon hang a left into the Loews 86th Street multiplex.

Good Lord. Was she meeting men in a movie theater? I suppose it was possible. I peered in the door and, sure enough, there she was in the ticket line. Not that there was a line for the evening show on a school night, but she was there, and as I looked she bought a ticket and headed for the escalator.

Oh, hell.

I went in, took a look. There were seven movies playing. I had no idea which one she bought, but it probably didn't matter. I got a ticket for the latest Matt Damon thriller and hurried to the escalator as rapidly as possible without drawing attention to myself. At the top an usher tore my ticket and let me into the concession area. I didn't buy popcorn. I looked around for my quarry, who was long gone.

Great. Seven films to choose from. I tried the one I had the ticket for, not that it mattered, no one was checking ticket stubs at the door. Once you bought admission, there was nothing to stop you from theater hopping. Which I proceeded to do.

Sharon was not servicing a john in the Matt Damon movie. Nor was she plying her trade in the one I tried next. Or the one after that.

In my case, sixth time was the charm. I came in the door, and there she was, sitting with two other girls who appeared to be approximately her age. A bevy of hookers? Had I stumbled on some high school sex club? Would the girls be joined by a bunch of old lechers?

They would not. As the previews gave way to the feature film, no one came near them. No one even seemed to be checking them out. Except me. I could imagine the projectionist watching me through the window, picking up the phone, and turning me in.

Up on the screen, a girl's heart was being broken because the boy she liked supposedly liked someone else, only he didn't, he really liked her, but it would take nearly two hours before the two of them figured that out. And as the plot slowly—and not nearly as amusingly as I'm sure all parties involved intended—unwound, it gradually dawned on me that I was being paid two hundred dollars to watch a chick flick.

It wasn't worth it.

11

MOMMY WAS APOLOGETIC. IT DIDN'T MAKE UP FOR THE chick flick, but after getting reamed out the day before, I wasn't unhappy to have an apologetic mom.

"She wasn't supposed to go to the movies."

"You mean she snuck out?"

"No, she just didn't tell us she was going. In advance, I mean. It was, 'Where you going, don't you have homework.' 'Done it, I'm going the movies, see you.'"

"That was okay with you?"

"It was better than other things she could have done. So, did you trace the car?"

"Just between you and me, I think the guy in the car is a dead end."

"So you didn't trace it?"

"I traced it."

I gave her the name and address.

"Is that all?"

"That's the only guy I traced."

"Surely you found out something about him."

"I did. He's got a wife and kid. He ought to be ashamed of himself."

"What's he do?"

"He's a congressman."

Her eyes widened. "That's perfect. That's just the type of leverage we need to put the screws on."

"For what? Odds are he's never gonna see your daughter again."

"I know. But . . ."

"But what?"

"I just wanna to be doing something."

"I don't know what you can do. Aside from sitting the girl down and having a good old-fashioned talk with her."

"I can't do that."

"So I gathered. And hubby mustn't know."

Jennifer took a breath. "Okay, here's the deal. Sharon's having a sleepover tonight. At a girlfriend's house. Or so she says. It could be true, it could be just a useful excuse. I want to find out which."

"How about calling the other girl's mother."

"I can't do that."

"Because it would be too simple and direct?"

"I don't want her to think I'm checking up on her."

"You think the mother would tattle?"

"I don't know what the mother would do. I don't want to put myself in someone else's hands. I want to do this myself."

"By which you mean you want me to do it."

"You don't want the job?"

I wanted the job. Despise me if you will, but I needed the money. I live in New York City, and rents aren't cheap, recession or no recession.

"What do you want me to do?"

"If she goes home with the girlfriend, fine. You can call it a day.

43

I don't expect you to sit through another movie. But if she goes somewhere else, in particular if she goes somewhere with an older man . . ."

"Yes?"

"I want you to bring her home."

"How do you expect me to do that?"

"You're the detective."

"I'm the private eye," I corrected. "I'm not the police detective. I have no authority. If she doesn't wanna come, I got no right to force her. And she isn't gonna wanna come."

"I don't care how you do it, just do it."

"The only way to do it is call you and have you come get her."

"I told you. That's not an option."

"Why not?"

"You wouldn't understand."

"Try me."

"There's more at stake here than you know. If you're not happy about it, I'm sorry. But I didn't hire you to make you happy. I've outlined the job. It's pretty straightforward. I want you to keep my daughter from getting hurt. How you do it is entirely up to you. Just leave us out of it."

She broke off, looked me right in the eye. "Now, you want the job?"

I should have just said no. Where was Nancy Reagan when I needed her? But there I was, the knight on his white horse, the stalwart protector of all young girls, and how was I going to refuse to help this one?

"Yes."

12

You ever carry an umbrella so it won't rain? I've done it. Not enough, clearly, for all the times I've come home drenched. In point of fact, I hate umbrellas, and would rather sprint up the block dodging raindrops than be caught with one. Just the way I would never wear my rubbers, which I considered using as an example, but rejected because of the double-entendre—I'm having enough problems with sex as it is. But if there was something that really mattered, something I really cared about, some occasion when I just didn't want it to rain, like my softball game, or Tommy's Little League game (Christ, is it only ball games?), I would bring along an umbrella on the theory that if I had it, it would forestall the event.

And more often than not it would work. Or maybe I just remember those times, having to carry the damn thing. Or was it Alice? There's a thought—maybe it was Alice, ridiculing me for taking an umbrella in the bright sunshine, which only Alice can imbue with the right amount of bemused tolerance or sympathetic condescension. Or maybe I'm just projecting.

Anyway, for the number of times it worked, as well as the times it didn't, the reassuring feel of the clumsy instrument clutched in my hesitant hand always eased the burden. At least until Alice did her thing.

Today, Alice wasn't there. Alice wouldn't notice if I took an umbrella. She wouldn't know unless I told her. Neither would MacAullif. Or Richard.

The minute I had those thoughts I wanted to tell Alice, MacAullif, and Richard. Wanted to ask their advice. Get their opinions on the weather. Did they think it would rain?

Of course, in all instances, I knew what that advice would be: You cannot let a client dictate terms. You are dealing with a cuckoo person. If you follow her instructions, *you* are a cuckoo person. No good can come of this. You need an intervention. A private eye sponsor. A twelve-step withdrawal from surveillance. The moment you get your first urge to do something not quite legal that a private eye on television might attempt, you need to activate your PI alarm. "Help. I've fallen for an investigative technique and I can't get up."

That doesn't quite work either as an example or as a comedy bit. Which is not surprising. My comedy routines never worked either. Yeah, I did stand-up. Only one of a number of failed careers, which included acting, writing, screenwriting, and songwriting, my stand-up career was perhaps the most abortive. My routines never went anywhere.

For instance, I once wrote a series of Man Most Likely jokes. Yeah, I know, you never heard of the Man Most Likely jokes. That's because there is no such thing. That's because I wrote it. The premise was the names of the people most likely to be associated with certain actions. For example: "The man climbing into the lion's cage is most likely to be Claude."

Doesn't that seem like a wonderful premise for a series of jokes? Short, clean, excellent setup, perfect payoff. The reason the routine never got anywhere was "The man climbing into the lion's cage is most likely to be Claude" was the only one I was ever able to come up with.

I know, I'm digressing horribly. The problem is, I didn't want to face the situation. Because, once again, my do-good, white knight nature, coupled with my horny as hell raging hormones, had allowed my client to seduce me, without the benefit of actual sex, but to lure me coquettishly into something that in my heart of hearts I knew I shouldn't be doing.

I would be following little Lolita on her journey from school. Which was kind of like a trip to Vegas. If she went home with her girlfriend, buzzers and bells would go off, lights would flash, gold bars would line up, and the slot machine would spit out two hundred dollars.

If she hopped into a car with somebody else, I would be mugged and dumped in the gutter.

Unlike Vegas, I wasn't betting a long shot. Surely, the odds favored her going home with a friend. However, there was a chance, albeit a small chance, that she wouldn't.

I needed an umbrella.

13

"I NEED A MICKEY FINN."

Fred Lazar looked at me like a total stranger, like he'd never seen me before. "I don't think I heard you right. In fact, I'm sure I didn't. Why don't you come in and try again."

"You got to help me, Fred. I'm in trouble."

"And misery loves company, so you'd like me in trouble too."

Fred was a stocky guy with a broken nose and a bulge under his arm. As much as I didn't look like a private eye, Fred did. Fred was the guy who got me into the private eye business way back when. I hadn't seen him much since then, for which he was grateful. Fred always regarded me as colossal fuckup for whom negligence work would be just about the limit of my expertise. At the time, he had been happy to steer me into a job that he didn't want.

"I don't know what you're up to, but slippin' someone a mickey is what happens in films. You always get in trouble when you work from films."

"This is a little different."

"Why?"

"I'm already in trouble. I'm trying to get out."

Fred tried to keep from asking, but it was too damn hard. "Why are you in trouble?"

I told him the story. He didn't look pleased. "You want to drug a teenage girl?"

"I don't want to drug her, no."

"Then why are you even considering this?"

"I'm not going to let some pervert on Viagra use her body for target practice."

"A noble sentiment."

"Which means I gotta get her away. The problem is, she won't want to come."

"Poor choice of words."

"Get your mind out of the gutter. She won't wanna go, so how can I bring her home?"

"That is a problem."

"Unless you wanna come with me. I bet you could take her."

"Sorry. Not my style."

"So I need a mickey."

"You know what a mickey is?"

"Yeah. Chloral hydrate. I had it once for an EEG."

"You had an EEG?"

"Yeah. They give you chloral hydrate to make you sleep."

"Why'd you have an EEG?"

"See if anything was going on."

"What did it show?"

"Unremarkable brain."

"I could have told you that *without* an EEG."

"Yeah, I know. Can you get it?"

"Chloral hydrate?"

"Yeah."

"This is a bad idea."

"I know that. You got a better one?"

"Not off the top of my head."

"So, it's either chloral hydrate, or you come with me." I shrugged, spread my arms. "Your choice."

14

HE SLIPPED ME A MICKEY. I DON'T MEAN HE PUT IT IN MY drink. I mean he put it in my pocket. And not then and there. It's not like he had it on him. But my phone rang two hours later and he hooked me up.

It wasn't cheap.

"Two hundred dollars? I don't want an EEG, just the drug."

"It might be cheaper at your local pharmacy. Why don't you give it a try."

"Yeah, but two hundred dollars."

"That's mostly bribe money. Want me to break it down?"

"No. Thanks, man."

So he slipped me a mickey. It was in a little tube with a stopper. The tube was hand-labeled BI.

"BI?"

"Bad idea."

Which is how I came to be hanging around outside a public

school with a tube of chloral hydrate in my pocket. It occurred to me if the cops picked me up and shook me down, I'd be hard-pressed to explain what I was doing there without betraying the confidence of a client. Even *with* betraying the confidence of a client I'd be on rather shaky ground.

I hung out down the block, tried to look inconspicuous. Try it sometime. I can give you a hint. Don't whistle nonchalantly. That's how the movies portray someone *trying* to look innocent. In other words, someone looking guilty. Just a hint, in case you ever find yourself outside a public school with tube of chloral hydrate in your pocket.

Today I got lucky. At 3:45 Sharon was out the door chatting happily with a girlfriend.

Great. God bless the umbrella. All my preparations were for naught. It's a jackpot. Or at least a wash. I'd earn my two hundred bucks for watching TV. On the other hand, I wouldn't charge 'em for the chloral hydrate. I'd break even and love it. After all, how often do you get out of Vegas breaking even?

Only they didn't go home. Go on kids. I gotta tail you to the sleepover. I got the address. You go there, I'm done. I haven't been enjoying this particular case. I'd like to hang it up.

Only they're not doing it. They're setting down their book bags and giggling to each other. What are they giggling about? Please tell me the other girl isn't a hooker too.

You wouldn't think so. Sharon's friend didn't look any more like a hooker than Sharon did. Straw-colored curly hair, itty-bitty button nose. Hell, she was chewing bubble gum. Say it ain't so, Joe.

Come on, kids. Pick up your book bags and go home.

They didn't do that. Instead they lined up shoulder to shoulder, and, on a given count, proceeded to perform synchro-nized movements.

They were cheerleaders. Practicing some god-awful routine with which to encourage testosterone-filled teenage boys to pummel each other on some playing field or other. Most likely football or soccer. Whatever the venue, that's what they were about.

I hate to be a mine's better, but mine was clearly better. Sharon had all the moves. Style, grace, she beat the other girl hands down.

I tried not to think whence such athleticism might have sprung.

The girls ran through three or four routines, stopping occasionally to clean up some move. I wondered what the cheerleading outfits were like. Cute, surely, in a sterile, nonsexy way.

A car horn honked.

Sharon grabbed her book bag, dashed to the curb.

My jaw tightened.

It was the Lexus I'd followed before. Congressman Jason Blake's car.

He wouldn't get away. This time I wasn't dependent on a passing cab. I had my own car double-parked up the block, screw the parking tickets. I'd either pass them on to the client or take the loss. The scumbag was mine.

I hurried down the block to my car. Amazingly, I hadn't gotten a ticket. I hopped in, fired her up, and by the time the Lexus had maneuvered around the buses I was ready to go. When he hit the corner, I was right on his tail.

The congressman hung a left, headed for home. Of course, that presented a problem. What did I do when he went into the underground garage? Here I was winging it. The only thing I could think of was to drive right in after him. I'd follow him to his parking space, block his car with mine, hop out, and say, "Okay, sleazebag, let's have a little talk."

It was an intriguing idea. What would he do then? Call the cops on me? I didn't think so. He wouldn't want to call the cops. Following him through the garage door was a rather attractive scenario. Unless it cut my car in half.

Only he didn't turn into his garage. That was pretty disappointing, once I had it worked out. But he went right on by his apartment house and on down Fifth Avenue.

The traffic got heavy in the Fifties due to the Broadway mall. Don't get me started. The city closed Broadway in the theater district to create a permanent pedestrian mall. The spillover traffic onto the nearest downtown avenues was enough to piss off even George M. Cohan, the man the mall honored.

We inched our way south of 42nd Street, hung a right on 37th, wove our way through the trucks in the garment district over to Seventh Avenue. I was still trying to figure out what the congressman was up to, when he hung a left into a garage. It wasn't a private garage. A huge sign flashed PARK. Below it proclaimed some astronomical daily rate in glowing block capitols as if it were the deal of the century.

I must admit, up until that point I had been working out other scenarios in my mind, charitable scenarios, ones that cast the congressman in a less odious light. Not the least of which was this: MacAullif said the congressman had a kid. Maybe that kid was a teenage son. Maybe that teenage son was old enough to drive. Maybe he was Sharon's friend, and maybe this was a perfectly innocent teenage date.

That pipe dream vanished when the sleazeball himself emerged from the car and handed the keys to the attendant. The garage was the valet parking type, where you left your car at the curb instead of driving it in yourself. The attendant handed Congressman Blake a parking ticket stub, and he and Sharon headed down the street.

Before the attendant could climb into the congressman's car, I pulled up behind it and hopped out.

"I'm in a hurry. Can you give me a ticket?"

He looked at me like, how big a hurry?

I whipped a twenty-dollar bill out of my pocket. "Please."

He grinned a snaggle-tooth at me, tore out the ticket, traded it for the bill.

I grabbed the ticket stub, headed down the block. I caught up with them at the next corner. They were waiting for the light. When it changed, they crossed Seventh Avenue.

They were heading for Madison Square Garden.

I frowned. What was at the Garden? It wasn't basketball or hockey season. They had rock concerts, yes, but there wasn't one on the marquee. So where were they going?

The mystery was solved when they went through the front door and headed downstairs. Madison Square Garden was above Penn Station.

They were taking a train.

I bought a ticket on the 5:00 P.M. Acela, which appeared to be the train they were taking. If it wasn't I was going to feel like a fool. But they bought their tickets at one of those automated Amtrak kiosks, and as near as I could tell that was what the congressman punched in.

In case you've never ridden Amtrak, the Acela is the faster, more expensive train. That figured.

In Penn Station there are two Amtrak waiting areas, the Acela waiting area, and the non-Acela waiting area. As near as I could tell, they are absolutely alike. But you have to show your ticket to get into them, and if you don't have an Acela ticket you can't get into the ritzy, Acela waiting area, and you have to sit with the unwashed masses in the other one, for all the difference it made.

Today, the segregated waiting areas actually served a purpose. If Congressman Blake got into the Acela waiting room, it would confirm the fact he had bought Acela tickets.

Just my luck, the son of a bitch didn't do it. Instead, he and Sharon stood in the middle of the station looking up at the huge departure board, where every ten or fifteen seconds the train names and departure times would whirl with a clack, clack, clack, and reappear in different positions, or sometimes the same position, it was not always clear which, unless you really cared about that particular train. The 5:00 Acela to Washington was the one I wanted to see clacking. My ticket was to Philadelphia, as I presumed their tickets were, but Philadelphia was one of a few stops on the line. Once the gate was posted, there would be a mad dash to the escalator to take you down to the track.

The congressman and the kid wandered off to the Hudson News shop to purchase something for their trip. A newspaper for him, a coloring book for her.

She actually bought a teen magazine. At least, that's what she had in her hand when the big board went clack, clack, clack, and the Washington Acela went 13E, which meant it would be departing from track 13 at the east gate, and there was a sudden stampede for the escalator in that direction. The congressman hissed at the kid to come on. She reluctantly left her magazine on the counter, went out, and got in line, which was good. I didn't want them at the end of the line. That would have made it hard for me to be behind them. I got in line about a dozen people back, showed my ticket at the gate, and hopped on the top of the escalator just as the congressman and the kid were nearing the bottom.

They followed the crowd toward the back of the train, the congressman pushing Sharon along as if he were the big grown-up and she were the naive kid who'd never ridden a train before. I wondered how much that carried over into their role playing.

I hit the bottom of the escalator and hoofed along after them. They went in a business class car, which was good, because that's the kind of ticket I had. I caught up, hopped onto the train.

I'd ridden the Acela before, so I knew what to expect. Nonetheless, I had envisioned something out of *North by Northwest*, with a sleeping car and a classy dining car where waiters served you cooling drinks at tables with cloth napkins, and handed you menus, as opposed to a café car that would microwave you a burger. If I was going to have a train adventure, that was what I wanted. Spies slipping notes to henchman in the next car.

But it was not to be. The car was your standard railroad train car, filled with seats. Granted, there were a few instances of seats facing backward with a table between them, making an alcove for four. Still, it was a wide open alcove, not behind closed doors like in *The Lady Vanishes*, my other railroad movie. Both directed by Alfred Hitchcock.

Well, it would have to do. This wasn't about me having a good time. It was about saving a girl from disaster without trashing my pitiful career.

There was an pair of empty seats halfway down the car. Naturally, they took them. Which presented a problem. I would have to find a seat further down the car. Which meant walking past them. Not that I expected the girl to recognize the back of my head. Even so. I kept my arm up, scratched my ear, covered my face as I went by.

Directly in front of them was an empty seat. Too close. Didn't want it. Would it look suspicious if I passed it by? Would I call attention to myself? Would suddenly every eye in the car be on me? People staring. Pointing. In amazement. In awe. In horror. *He didn't take the seat! That man didn't take the seat! Mommy, Mommy, I'm scared!*

I kept going. No alarms went off. No bells and whistles. I flopped into another empty seat a little way down the car. Perfect.

Except it was on the same side as they were. I couldn't peer at them diagonally across the aisle. To see them, I would have to peek over the top of my seat. And I wouldn't see them. I would see the people directly behind me. Which would have fine if I'd sat in the seat directly in front of them but which wouldn't work now. Should I get up and go back? Should I look for a seat across the aisle? Should I consider another line of work?

I was still contemplating my options when the train pulled out of the station. That was a relief. I was afraid someone would come and sit next to me. I would have to explain that I needed the aisle seat. I would have to give some reason other than surveillance. Why do you need an aisle seat on a train? Particularly, an Acela Express, where the stations are far apart. It's not like I'd be getting right off. So what could I plead? Acute and chronic diarrhea. There's a romantic image. Just the sort of thing to tell the young lady who sat down with you. Perfect for the secret agent. "Bond. James Bond. I poop a lot."

The conductor came around and punched my ticket. Unfortunately, he didn't say, "Ah, Philadelphia. Just like the couple six rows back." On the other hand, he didn't recognize me as the man wanted for murder at the UN.

Fifteen minutes later we stopped in New Jersey and more people got on. I was sitting on the aisle, so if anyone wanted the seat they would have to climb over me or ask me to move. No one did. The train pulled out of the station. The conductor came down the aisle, quicker this time since most tickets were already punched and he only had to deal with the few passengers who just got on.

I sat and stewed. Wished I'd brought a newspaper, or a book, or a crossword puzzle, or a Sudoku, or a KenKen.

After the conductor went by I had a flash of panic. What if they got off. When everyone else got on, they got off, and here I was, riding a train to Philadelphia with my quarry on the loose in Newark, New Jersey. Which would not be apt to earn me the PI of the Month award.

It was ridiculous, of course. No one takes an Acela for one fifteen-minute stop. It's an expensive, high-speed train. You don't pay the premium to save the potential one to two minutes over the local train.

But what if you did it to throw off your tail?

Bullshit. He doesn't know he's wearing a tail.

Unless he spotted you. After all, he's being followed by the world's least competent detective.

I stifled such thoughts. Tried to calm myself with cool rationale. Told myself I was an obsessive, compulsive, paranoid fool. That wasn't as calming as I'd hoped. Nonetheless, the idea I was being silly hit home. *They're right there. You can check on them if you want, but they're right there.*

I knew that was true. They were right there, and I didn't have to check on them.

I had to check on them.

I needed a plausible excuse to walk past them. Was the café car in that direction? Was the bathroom at that end of the car?

Moron. No one's going to stop you and ask where you're going. Just get up and go.

I slid from my seat, started up the aisle. As I did, a sudden fear gripped me.

What if they're making out?

If they were making out, as I was terribly afraid they might be, I couldn't ignore it. I would have to do something about it. I would grab the son of a bitch and pull him off her. Which would be an utter disaster. Aside from blowing my cover, I'm no fighter, and he would beat the shit out of me. Of course, he'd have some explaining to do to the cops. Even so, it was not the way I wanted to spend my afternoon. But if they were making out, I was gonna do it.

They weren't making out. He was reading the newspaper. She was doing her homework.

It killed me, her doing her homework. Just like practicing cheerleading. All the normal little girl things broke my heart.

I kept going, reached the end of the car.

Okay, now what? Go to the men's room? Go to the café car? Go back? Stay here?

I didn't want to go back to my seat, but I didn't want to stand up for the rest of the trip. Could I walk back in the other direction without having accomplished any useful purpose?

Absolutely. No one was looking at me. No one would know.

Cool. Secret Agent fakes out passengers, walks length of car.

Oh, the tiny victories.

I walked back past the congressman and the kid. Reached my seat and kept going. I didn't want to sit there again. I wasn't happy there.

A few rows down was an empty seat on the other side. I slid into it and looked back up the aisle. Excellent. From there I could see if they left their seats. Of course, I had to turn around and crane my neck, but it was possible. It occurred to me that if were a woman, I'd have a makeup mirror I could angle and watch the aisle without turning around.

Of course, I'd also have breasts.

I wondered if I could keep from staring at them.

15

THEY GOT OFF IN PHILADELPHIA.

They were closer to the back of the car, so they went out that way, which was good, it put me behind them. Of course, if they'd come my way, I would have just scrunched down until they went by and wound up behind them anyway. Still, I was at the point where I was appreciating anything in my favor.

Outside the station was a taxi waiting line.

Shit. No way that worked. In order to get a taxi in time to follow them, I'd have to be right behind them, and they'd see me. If I was any further back in line, by the time the dispatcher got me a cab, they'd be long gone.

I ignored the taxi line, walked in the direction from which the cabs came. I hit the street just as a cab was about to turn in. I stepped in front of it. The driver hit his brakes, honked his horn, and cursed.

In a flash I was at the driver's window. "I need a cab. Twenty bucks says this one's mine."

"I could get fined."

"Forty. Last offer."

The driver looked at me. "Hop in."

"Drive by, pull up where the cabs pull out, stop there."

"I don't want no trouble."

"I'm not giving you trouble. I'm giving you cash." I whipped out my license, flashed it in his face. "I'm a private eye, I'm tailing a guy and a girl. No rough stuff. For you it's all gravy."

The cabbie stopped at the exit. I opened the door, stood, half in, half out, in case the son of a bitch tried to drive off. The congressman and the girl were now fourth. With a steady stream of taxis lining up, it was only a minute and a half before the starter ushered them into one and slammed the door.

"That's them. Don't lose 'em, but don't let 'em know we're following them."

"No rough stuff."

"None."

My cab pulled out, dropped in behind theirs.

I sat bolt upright in the backseat, tried to keep from telling my cabbie he was getting too close, or, alternately, letting them get away.

We drove down Independence Mall and took a lap around the Liberty Bell. I wondered if he was showing her the sights. I couldn't imagine he would care.

We were heading out of town, which didn't make sense, but none of this made sense. Spending a bundle for a hooker, you'd think you'd rather spend your time in bed, rather than tooling around the country. I mean, New York or Philadelphia, it's the same girl, what's the big deal?

A short way out in the suburbs we pulled into the huge parking lot of the Show Palace.

Show Palace?

If he was putting her to work in a girlie joint, I was setting my speed dial for MacAullif. I didn't care if he had jurisdiction here or not, he knew people, he could make some calls. By God, I'd shut down the place.

Only it didn't appear to be a titty bar, at least from the clientele. There were as many women as men, maybe more, and a lot of them were young. Maybe not as young as Sharon, but pretty damn young. What the hell was going on?

I found out at the door.

It was a dinner theater. With some pop singer performing. Along the lines of Celine Dion, but not as famous. I knew her name vaguely, couldn't match a face or a song to it.

I gave them a ten-second head start, then followed them in.

A woman batted false eyelashes and smiled too much lipstick at me. "One? Fine. Dinner's a hundred dollars minimum. You pay in advance, your waiter will charge you the balance. Cash or credit card?"

I wanted to pay by credit card with a receipt for my client, only if I did that, they'd be long gone. I fished out five twenties, handed them over.

Before I could follow the congressman, a young waiter, attracted by the sound of my money, appeared at my elbow to guide me through the front door.

Inside was a spacious dining room, a bit of an optical illusion, appearing way too large for the size of the building. The stage on which the pop singer would perform was about a mile from the door. There were hundreds of tables, some for two, some for four. I was guided to a table for one, which was actually a stool by a pillar, but what do you expect for a hundred bucks? I didn't care. I wasn't staying there anyway. I accepted a menu while my eyes probed the semidarkness for the congressman and the kid.

I spotted them weaving their way through the tables in the direction of the restrooms. I stood my menu up on my table like an open book, and took off after them.

They didn't go into the bathrooms. They went right on by

toward an unmarked door at the end of the corridor. A burly, tattooed skinhead stood next to the door. The congressman
approached him, said the magic word, and the Hell's Angel
wannabe opened the door and let them in.

My mind was churning a mile a minute. Backstage? He's taking
her backstage? To meet a pop star diva? A kinky pop star diva?
What had the congressman got going on? Or, worse still, was the
girl a mere bargaining chip, something to throw to the roadies
while he got it on with the chanteuse? If that's what she was.
Could a pop star be a chanteuse? What the hell was a chanteuse
anyway? Why am I throwing around words I don't understand—
trying to appear more intellectual than I am? I should be going old
school, tough guy private eye long about now. Kneeing the roadie
in the nuts and walking through the door, cool as ice.

I wandered in that direction, just to see what would happen.
The minute I passed the men's room door, the roadie's nose
twitched, like a dog on guard who just smelled an intruder. Actually, a bad move on his part. It made me conscious of my own nose,
and the air, and what it smelled like. And coming from the direction of the door was the unmistakable odor of marijuana.

Great. Something else to bust the congressman for. Now I had
him on sex and drugs. I wondered when he was up for re-election.
The guy might have a hard time.

I walked down the hall. Three hundred pounds of tattooed
roadie blocked the door.

"What do you want?"

"Could I get in there?"

"What?"

"I was wondering if I could go inside."

"Who are you?"

"I'm a fan."

"Get lost."

"You let those other people in."

"They got a right to be there."

"How come?"

He opened his mouth, closed it. Scowled. "None of your business. Get the hell out of here. What are you, a reporter? If you're a reporter, wait in the autograph line like everybody else."

"I'm not a reporter."

"Then you got no reason to be here. Go on. Run along."

I went back to my table, kept an eye on the door. The waiter came over, asked me if I'd like a drink. I ordered a Diet Coke. He wasn't pleased. It would take a lot of Diet Cokes to earn out my hundred-dollar minimum.

They were out in twenty minutes. I sized up the kid, tried to see if she looked any the worse for wear. She didn't. Just a schoolgirl, toting a book bag. She wasn't giggling like she'd been smoking grass. Of course, I wasn't too up on what a teenager smoking grass acted like. I hadn't even seen any of the stoner movies. I only knew the half of Harold and Kumar that was on *House*. Nonetheless, if she was buzzed, I would have expected some difference. She did seem a little exhilarated. I don't recall marijuana producing exhilaration. A goofy, mellow groove, not an upper. Or so I hear.

Sharon and Congressman Blake returned to their table, which was not that far from mine, but closer to the stage, which was good in that they'd be looking in that direction, whereas I'd be looking at them.

The congressman signaled the waiter over, gave him an order. Eager to use up his two hundred bucks, no doubt.

When the waiter left they picked up the large leather-bound menus on the table. I had one on mine but hadn't paid any attention to it. That's because I never took the advance course on private eye surveillance about appearing natural in a restaurant by pretending you were there to eat.

I picked up the menu, flipped it open, so if a waiter appeared I'd be ready. I could place my order without taking my eyes off the congressman and the kid. I took a look at the entrees. The rib-eye looked good. At sixty-five bucks it would take a whack out of the hundred-dollar deposit. What the hell. I was hungry. Might as well use it up.

And for starters, a pear salad, with shaved reggiano and balsamic vinaigrette, for a mere eighteen ninety-five. Throw in tax and the Diet Coke, and my waiter might start liking me again.

My waiter seemed in no hurry to take my order. He reappeared with my Diet Coke, plunked it on the table, and was gone before I could ask him about the day's specials. Not that I was going to, but even so.

I wondered how many tables the guy was covering. Not the congressman and the kid. Their waiter was back with a tray from which he delivered the congressman a martini, and the kid . . . a margarita!

Oh, the charges were adding up.

Sharon sipped her drink, giggled, licked salt off the rim of her glass.

I wondered if they carded anyone in this place. Or if she just got by because she was with the congressman. I wondered if he was a regular. That would make sense. He was allowed backstage. He was allowed to order booze for his pubescent date. After smoking dope, no doubt.

The waiter came back, asked me if I'd made up my mind. I hadn't, really. I was torn between ordering the rib-eye and breaking the congressman's nose. It was a tossup, really. I mean, the rib-eye sounded good, but the thought of hearing that nose crack . . .

I stifled the urge, ordered salad and the steak.

"How would you like it cooked?"

"If I say rare, what will I get?"

"Rare is bloody. Medium rare is red. Medium is pink."

"I guess I tend toward medium."

The waiter repeated "tend toward medium" as if he were writing it down. More likely, "asshole, burn it."

"Would you like another Diet Coke?"

I'd barely touched the one I had. "Not just yet."

As the waiter hurried off in quest of fresher game, I realized my attention had been diverted momentarily from the congressman and the kid. There was a waiter at their table too, going through a similar routine, though probably with more deference. He seemed quite happy with what he was writing. Probably "big tipper, remember to smile."

The waiter's routine ended with a gesture toward their drinks.

Sharon's margarita was half gone. She nodded yes. The congressman shook his head.

Son of a bitch. Staying sober while plying her with booze. I wondered why. Was there anything he wanted she wouldn't do? Something particularly kinky, perhaps? Which would explain the elaborate preparations, the trip, the dope, the booze.

Sort of.

The lights went down, and the performance began.

It wasn't the singing star. It was her opening act. Some god-awful boy band I'd never heard of, no doubt aping some god-awful boy band I'd heard of vaguely but hadn't a clue who they actually were. They didn't play instruments, just sang and danced, if that's what you could call it, or at least moved in unison. They had short hair, huge smiles, wore matching slacks and polo shirts.

They made me wish I hadn't ordered dinner. Perhaps I'm just jealous. Perhaps I just wished I were one of them. Young and successful, singing for a roomful of people. Instead of conducting a sordid clandestine surveillance.

The song ended. Sharon was cheering, wildly, enthusiastically, almost spilling her drink. Her second drink. Which I noticed was almost gone.

The congressman surreptitiously motioned the waiter over, pointed to her glass. The waiter smiled and nodded.

So what was I going to do? I couldn't sit here and watch him pour booze down her throat all night. And I couldn't bear much more of the Backside Street Boys. I had to get her out of there.

I got to my feet, wove my way through the tables in their direction. Weighed my chances. I had the disadvantage that she knew me. The advantage: she must be pretty drunk.

Plus she was watching the stage. The boys were performing another nauseating step-in-time routine, which, from the way she was paying attention, must have been absolutely fascinating.

I stumbled against their table. Put out my hand to brace myself. Actually knocked over their salt shaker. Muttered, "Sorry, sorry," and stumbled away.

I didn't look behind me. If the congressman was coming to beat my brains in, I didn't want to know. If a waiter was coming to escort me from the dining room, I didn't want to know that either. I just wanted to put as much distance between me and the congressman's table as possible.

That and screw the top back on what was left in my bottle of chloral hydrate.

She had another drink after that. The girl clearly had an iron constitution. She probably didn't weigh more than a hundred pounds soaking wet, and here she was, guzzling margarita after margarita with enough chloral hydrate in her to fell a bull moose. Had I missed her glass? Poured it all over the table?

I had not. Just as the boy band was leaving the stage to thunderous applause, which I could fully understand (I was delighted to see them go too), she folded her arms on the table, leaned forward, and put her head down, just as if it were nap time in school.

The congressman peered at her curiously. He couldn't know she'd been drugged. With all the booze she'd had, he must have thought she'd just passed out. He poked her, tried to rouse her, but no luck.

If he asked the waiter to call a doctor, I was sunk. But I didn't think he would. He wouldn't want to explain to some medic why the sixteen-year-old girl he was sitting with in a nightclub was sloshed to the gills.

The congressman checked to see if she was breathing, a point in his favor—and there were damn few—and headed in the direction of the restrooms. More likely he was going backstage, to tell the diva there'd been a slight hitch in his plans.

I watched him disappear down the hall, then snagged a passing waiter, neither mine nor theirs. "Help me, please! My daughter's sick!"

"What?"

I pointed. "My daughter. Over there. She's sick. I think she's going to throw up."

The waiter, a young dude with a pointy headed haircut, was eager to pass the buck. "Hey, man, that's not my table."

"Come on, help me get her out of here. It'd be better if she throws up in the parking lot. Please."

He smelled a tip. "Okay, man."

With his help, I lifted Sharon up from the table, put her arm around my neck. "Take the other side."

The waiter did. Once he'd agreed to do it, the guy was actually getting off on being a hero. He led us through the tables, saying, "Excuse us, please. Sick customer coming through."

Glancing over my shoulder I saw the congressman coming back. Damn. Why couldn't he stay for a joint? He'll reach the table and raise the alarm.

No, he won't. He'll assume she came to and went to the bathroom.

But then he would have passed her.

What the hell *will* he assume?

Will he hear the words "sick customer," and put two and two together?

Why should he? Surely people's lives aren't so dreary they'd still be discussing our impromptu exit.

Damn. How big was this fucking room? Where the hell's the door?

We reached it, went through the lobby, outside, and down the front steps.

I stuck a twenty in his hand. "Thanks, man. Get back to you tables. I can take it from here."

He grinned and left.

The doorman, attracted by the size of the bill, came over. "Need some help?"

"I need a cab. Can you get me one?"

"Where to?"

"Thirtieth Street Station."

"Car service would be cheaper."

"I don't care what's cheaper, just what's quicker. My daughter's sick. I want to get her in a cab."

"Wait right here."

The doorman ran out in the street, blew his whistle like he was a referee calling the most flagrant foul in the history of the NBA.

A taxi in the passing lane slammed on its brakes, cut off a bus, and swerved in the entrance.

I slipped the doorman a bill, which was not lost on the cabby, and hopped in. The doorman slammed the door, and the cab took off.

Through the rear window I could see the congressman appear in the door of the nightclub.

He didn't look happy.

16

EVER HANG AROUND A TRAIN STATION WITH AN UNCONSCIOUS girl? It's not all it's cracked up to be. Aside from the strong possibility of being mistaken for the very pervert you're attempting to save her from, there is also the simple logistical problem of keeping her upright. The damn benches don't have sides. Or arms. Or anything to lean a young girl against in order to keep her from slumping sideways, or keeling over on the floor, a dead giveaway that something is wrong.

I managed to prop her up while I bought a ticket. Two tickets, actually. Expenses were adding up. I hoped Mama wouldn't be mad.

I sat down next to Sharon, put her book bag in her lap, angled her head in the right direction, and acted out a scenario in which the parent is lecturing the stubborn child, who has closed her eyes and is pretending not to listen. I doubt if it fooled anyone. On the other hand, I doubt if anyone was paying attention.

Meanwhile, I kept watching the door, in case the congressman should burst in. Which I fully expected to happen. It didn't, which confused me. What was wrong with the perverts today? No resolve, no gumption. Damned if I'd ever vote for him again.

The light blinked for our train. I held Sharon up, walked her through the gate.

This was the part where the guy checking tickets says, "All right, buddy, what you trying to pull?" He didn't. We sailed right through, Sharon teetering on wobbly legs like a seasoned pro.

I had a little trouble getting her up the steps of the train, but no one was looking. At least no one in authority. I got her up, marched her in, found a seat, sat her down. Propped her up against the window, peered out to see if any congressmen were running down the track. None were.

"Go to sleep, I'll wake you up when we get there," I said for the benefit of no one in particular.

I wondered how long it would take the drug to wear off. I had a little more, if I needed it, but I didn't know how I'd get her to swallow it. When I had my EEG I think I slept about an hour. Maybe more. Times flies when you're asleep. Try as I would, I couldn't dredge up an accurate assessment of how long I'd been out.

I had an image of a cartoon character: every time the girl stirs you bop her over the head with a wooden hammer. Probably not a good move. I didn't have a wooden hammer. Passengers might look at me funny if I tried to borrow one.

We'd just stopped at a station when the girl woke up. I don't think she saw anything. Or if she did, she didn't comprehend it. If she saw me, she'd scream. So, even if her eyes were delivering a picture, her brain wasn't processing it.

While I was trying to figure out how to handle her, she passed out again. Some days you get lucky. This was one of them. She slept all the way to New York.

I marched her off the train right onto the escalator and up to the waiting room. From there it was just a long, long city block through an indoor row of shops to Seventh Avenue and the street.

There was an officer right outside Penn Station. I was sure he'd arrest me. He didn't. He looked at me in a bemused fashion when I walked by with the girl. I was tempted to take his badge number. I stifled the urge.

I wrestled the girl across the street, propped her up against a lamppost, fished my wallet out of my pocket, found the parking stub.

Five minutes later I had my car.

I considered strapping Sharon in the front seat with a seatbelt. Decided against it. Not unless I wanted a teenage bobblehead. With my luck, I'd snap her neck. I opened the rear door, flopped her down on the back seat. If the garage attendant thought that was weird, he didn't say so, just accepted the dollar tip with all the disgust a piker of my ilk deserved. I couldn't help it. I was running low on cash.

I hopped in the car and drove away with an air of satisfaction.

I had done it.

I'd rescued the girl.

17

I PULLED UP NEXT TO A FIREPLUG ON THE CORNER, WHIPPED out my cell phone, made the call.

Luckily, I got Mommy. I don't know what I would have done if I'd gotten Daddy.

"I have your daughter," I said.

There was a sharp intake of breath. When she spoke, her voice was strained. "Is she all right?"

"Yes, of course."

"She's not hurt?"

"Don't be silly. Is your husband there?"

"Yes."

"If you don't want him to know, you'd better come outside."

She started to answer, then broke off suddenly as if the phone had been wrenched from her fingers.

A male voice said, "If you hurt my daughter, I will kill you! Do you hear me?"

"I hear you. No one's hurt your daughter. Just calm down."

"You have her with you?"

"Yes, I do."

"She's all right?"

"Yes, she is."

"I want to talk to her."

"She can't talk to you right now. You can talk to her when she gets home."

"How do I know she's all right?"

"I'm telling you she's all right. If you don't believe me, come see for yourself."

"If you won't let me talk to her, how do I know you even have my daughter?"

"Well, it would be a pretty stupid bluff if I didn't."

"All right. If you really have Sharon, where did you find her?"

"At a nightclub in Philly."

"You picked her up there?"

"That's right."

"How did you get her to come with you?"

"I'd rather not discuss it on the phone."

"I'll bet you wouldn't. Look here, I'm not playing games. I want my daughter back."

"I brought her back."

"But you won't tell me how, and she can't talk on the phone."

"Phones aren't safe. Particularly cell phones. You should know that. Look, you're wasting time. You want your daughter, come out and get her."

"Where are you?"

"In my car."

"Is Sharon with you?"

"Yes."

"Put her on the phone."

I took a breath. "I don't know what kind of power trip you're on, but this is ridiculous. Do you want your daughter or not?"

"How much?"

"What?"

"How much money do you want?"

"How much money do I want?"

"Don't play games. I'm not in the mood. How much do you want for her?"

"You're worried about money at a time like this?"

"I don't have that much on me. We can go to an ATM. How much do you want?"

"We're not going to an ATM. There's no need. Though this will be a little more costly than you might imagine."

Things happened fast.

The front door of my car flew open. Hands grabbed my arm. My cell phone flew from my fingers. I was wrenched from my seat with such force I could feel my arm dislocating itself from my shoulder, a searing pain that rocked my body and scattered whatever was left of my wits. Before I knew what was happening, I was slammed facedown over the hood of my car, the hard metal threatening to undo my dentist's attempts to save what little was left of my teeth. Pressure from all sides squashed me to the hood like a bug. My chest pressed down, my arms jerked backward and up, and my legs kicked apart as if I was about to be sodomized by a bull moose. Before I could take that in I was wrenched to my feet again, spun around by what proved to be a gaggle of uniformed cops, who shoved me into the back of a patrol car and slammed the door.

18

THE DETECTIVE WORE A SUIT AND TIE AND A PERPETUAL scowl. I've seen angry men before, but Detective Coleman was something special. He looked like he'd been born on the wrong side of the bed and was determined to make everyone pay for it. All in all, he didn't fit in with the detectives I knew. They were homicide detectives. They might be embittered, sarcastic, hard as nails, but there was one thing they didn't have that Detective Coleman seemed to. A holier-than-thou attitude. A contempt for the scum of the earth with which they dealt. Not that homicide cops don't despise perps—they do, but not with the same sense of loathing. A cop can respect a clever killer, in a way. Well, not really, but you get the idea. And Coleman wasn't like that.

So I didn't peg Coleman for homicide.

I pegged him for vice.

Coleman spun a chair around, sat down opposite me in the interrogation room. I was glad there was a table between us.

"All right, numbnuts," he said. "Why'd you grab the girl?"

"You're making a mistake."

"You didn't grab the girl? You didn't slip her a dose of chloral hydrate and put her in your car?"

"Would that be a crime?"

"I'm not here to answer questions, you are."

"Not if you phrase 'em that way. I'm here to cooperate. I'm not here to take the fall for any crime, technical or otherwise, that you might feel I have committed. Now, you want to stop the insinuating questions and discuss what happened, or you want to go at this adversarial?"

Coleman practically growled. "I'll ask any questions I want. I don't think you understand the situation here, or you wouldn't be cracking wise."

"I'm not cracking wise. I'm trying to get through this conversation without calling my lawyer because he won't be happy to hear from me. And you won't be happy to hear from him. If Richard gets involved, this will be unpleasant."

"Unpleasant? You don't think abduction's unpleasant?"

"You're charging me with abduction?"

"No one's charging anyone with anything. We're having a discussion here. I'd like to know how you came to grab the girl."

"Again, I don't like the phrasing."

"Oh, you don't? The girl was drugged in the back of your car. How'd she come to get there?"

"I'm not charged with anything?"

"No, you're not."

"So I could walk out of here right now."

"No, you couldn't."

"If I'm not charged with anything, you can't hold me."

"Then I'll charge you with something. If that's the way you wanna go. I thought you were innocent and wanted to clear this up."

"Exactly."

"So, what's this talk about being a hardass and walking out?"

"You're treating me like a perp. You wanna have a discussion, fine. I'll tell you exactly what happened."

"Let's hear it."

I told him about Sharon's mom hiring me to keep tabs on the girl. I left out any cars the girl might have hopped into, and Mom's suspicions regarding same. I also left out sitting in the movie theater watching a chick flick. Somehow, it didn't seem relevant.

Coleman waited impatiently through the narration. "That's all very interesting background, but could you tell me about today?"

"This is where we need to have a little understanding."

"What do you mean, a little understanding?"

"That you're treating me like a human being and not like a perp. If we're a couple of guys having a talk, I would have no problem. If you're a cop trying to pin something on me, I have to watch my step."

I had to hand it to Coleman. His wide-eyed, credulous, mocking tone was pitch-perfect. "You want me to promise if you're very good and tell me everything I'll let you go?"

"If you really mean it. Cross your heart and hope to die."

"Not my style. But I wouldn't worry about it. I'm not going to try to pin anything on you unless you've done something wrong. Of course you wouldn't do that."

"Naturally."

"So why don't you tell me what you did."

"This is the part my wife hates."

He frowned. "What?"

"Talking hypothetically. She hates it when I talk hypothetically."

"I wouldn't like it much, either."

"Yeah, but that's where we are. What with you refusing to promise, and all. So let's play what-if. What if Sharon's mother was afraid she was getting into trouble and hired me to get her out?"

"Are you saying that's what happened?"

"I'm saying what-if."

"Say some more."

"Suppose I knew that Sharon was involved with people who might want to take advantage of her."

"Suppose that were the case. What then?"

"She's a young girl. I'm an old fart. How would I get her to come with me?"

"Particularly since she didn't know who you were."

My eyes flicked. If I were a woman, one might have thought I'd looked at my breasts.

He caught it, naturally. That's what cops do. "Oh? She *did* know you?"

I sighed. "She didn't *know* me. I tried to pull a Peter Falk on her. You know, *Scared Straight*."

He frowned. "What the hell is that?"

Oh, hell. Shoot me now. My arresting officer was too young for me. "I'm a total stranger. I spoke to her on the street. Tried to put the fear of God in her, scare her into going home."

"Gee, did that work?"

"No. It was a bad move. They can't all be winners."

"No, they can't. So, when you saw her today, she might not have known you, but she knew you as the man who accosted her in the street."

I suddenly realized we had taken the conversation out of the realm of the hypothetical.

I smiled. "Nice try. I knew that *if* I ran into her today, she would not take kindly to me or be inclined to listen to anything I had to say. She would certainly not want to come home with me."

"I can understand that. Go on."

I shrugged. "Under the circumstances, it's possible the only way to extract her from people who might wish to do her harm, without the use of physical force, would be to do something to make her more cooperative."

"Like slip her chloral hydrate?"

"That would probably do that trick."

"Is that what you did?"

"Would that be a crime?"

"I'd have to look at the statute books."

"You do that and get back to me."

Coleman scowled. I couldn't tell if he was thinking up his next question or debating whether to jump over the table and rip my head off.

He chose the former. "Okay, you refuse to admit to drugging the girl and dragging her home, despite the fact she was found drugged in the back of your car. On the other hand, you claim you were hired to do so."

I said nothing.

"Isn't that right?"

"I was not hired to drug her. I *was* hired to bring her home."

"Uh-huh."

Coleman got up, opened the door, and gestured down the hall.

A plainclothes policewoman ushered in Sharon's father. I never met the man, but I recognized him at once from his wild-eyed, let-me-at-the-son-of-a-bitch look. It was all the policewoman could do to hold him back. At the risk of sounding sexist, I wish he'd been brought in by a police*man*. A large policeman. Possibly two.

"You animal!" he snarled. "You miserable scum!"

"I know how you feel, Mr Weldon," Coleman said. "But I need you to calm down, control yourself, answer some questions. Did you hire this man to bring back your daughter?"

"Absolutely not. I never saw him before in my life."

Coleman turned to me. "Well?"

"That's right. I never met the man. I was hired by his wife. All my dealings were with her."

Coleman turned to the woman I presumed was a plainclothes cop. "Is that right, Mrs. Weldon? Did you hire this man?"

81

19

RICHARD WASN'T HAPPY. FIRST OFF, BECAUSE NO ONE WAS dead. Richard doesn't like me to call him for legal advice unless it's a homicide. It's sort of his litmus test. If it's a murder, he's in. If it isn't, he's out. He made an exception this time due to the extent of the charges and the very real chance I might be convicted of some of them, which would put a crimp in my working for him. Richard counts on me more than he'd care to admit, largely because he can't find another investigator who can take the boredom of the job more than a couple of months. He's had a slew of temporaries, of varying degrees of intelligence and skill, not that the job requires much. Still, the employee must actually do it, a concept some of them are slow to grasp. Anyway, Richard saw my future at the firm in danger and made an exception to the rule.

"And just what has my client allegedly done?"

"Well," Coleman said, "he's admitted to—"

"Admitted? What an ugly word. I can't imagine my client

admitting to anything. That would be confoundedly stupid, even for him. I'm going to have to assume that you have misinterpreted something my client said that may have been injudicious, but certainly not criminal."

"Your client drugged and kidnapped an underage girl and drove her across the state line. We don't know what advantage he took of her while she was in that condition, but he certainly had the opportunity."

"My client says he did all this?"

"Actually, he tried to lie his way out of it. Which is another charge. Perjury. Obstruction of justice."

Richard grimaced. "The problem with you cops is you don't know the law. Let me straighten you out. In the first place, perjury and obstruction of justice aren't the same charge, they're two separate ones. Perjury is lying under oath. Did you put my client under oath? I find that hard to believe. Did he swear to tell the truth, the whole truth, and nothing but the truth, with the avowed intention of lying to you? That would seem a rather poor strategy, don't you think? No, perjury won't hold water. And obstruction of justice. What justice is he obstructing? If I understand it correctly, the charge in question involves bringing a girl home to her parents. I was not aware this was a crime. But I am certainly going to spend some time with the law books, just in case my knowledge of the subject is not as extensive as yours."

Coleman looked at Richard as if the attorney were something he might scrape off his shoe. "Just a minute. I'll get someone who speaks your language."

Coleman brought back an ADA who not only spoke Richard's language but shared his competitive spirit. ADA Fairfield was young and ambitious. Also attractive. ADA Fairfield was a woman. A nicely proportioned woman. Which is all I had to say on the subject. I was already in trouble.

"Now, then," she said, "let me be sure I've got this straight. I've got your client dead to rights on kidnapping, transporting a minor across state lines for immoral purposes, possession of an illegal substance, distribution of an illegal substance, extortion, and unlawful imprisonment. That's in addition to the obstruction of justice Detective Coleman seems concerned with. In light of which, I find it hard to believe you're giving us a hard time. Most attorneys in that situation would want to keep their heads down."

She smiled, and actually batted her eyes at him.

My mouth fell open.

Oh, my God. Didn't this one know anything? You didn't flirt with Richard. Richard would tear her a new one.

But he didn't. He said, "Well, it's easy to get the wrong impression. Stanley is my employee, as well as my client, and I have to tell you, he doesn't have the brains or the guts to do any of those things."

"Why do you employ him?"

"He's marginally competent, and willing to do the job. Usually, people bright enough to do it don't want it."

"Please. You'll turn my head. Did you come here to defend me, or beat up on me?"

The attractive ADA spoke to Richard as if I weren't there. "You doing this pro bono?"

"If I don't keep him out of jail, he can't do the work."

She smiled. "Maybe I can help you out. Your client has a bad case of the lies and hypotheticals. The things he states as facts are lies. The things that might be true, he presents as hypothetical."

"That sounds about right," Richard said. "Perhaps I can interpret. Of course, I only know what my client says, and, as you point out, much of that is suspect. But how about you let me take a whack at it."

She smiled. "Whack away."

I think Richard was nearly blushing. "It is my understanding, which may well be wrong, that my client was under the impression that the girl's mother had hired him to bring her back. It would appear that she has not. Largely due to the fact the woman who hired him was not actually the girl's mother. In other words, he was duped. Hard to imagine, from looking at him."

I shifted uncomfortably in my seat, waited to hear anything in my favor.

"Apparently, someone posed as the girl's mother, convinced my client her daughter was being led into a web of sin, and hired him to bring her back. I say apparently, because, under the circumstances, no one is admitting anything at this juncture. But here's the point. Regardless of who hired him, it appears that my client has uncovered an improper relationship between the young girl and a married man. A pillar of the community. A congressman, no less. And when that person transported the girl across the state line for immoral purposes, and plied her with drugs and alcohol, my client saved her from her fate, and brought her home to her parents."

"From whom he demanded money," ADA Fairfield pointed out.

"Train tickets to Philadelphia. A cover charge at a night club. Plus various bribes and gratuities."

"Which your client shelled out in order to wrest this girl away from the married man who had abducted her?"

"You don't think that's a good enough reason? I've seen gratuities approved that are listed simply 'Research.'"

"No problem with that, if they actually were for research. The problem here is your client is claiming payment for something he hasn't done."

"I beg your pardon?"

"Rescuing a young girl from the clutches of a married man. Apparently, that never happened."

"The hell it didn't! Who says that?"

"Stanley!" Richard said sharply. "My client speaks when he should listen." He smiled. "I sound like Don Corleone in *The Godfather*. Remember, in the scene with Sonny and Sollozzo? Or are you too young for that?"

Oh, my God. Was this standard lawyer maneuvering, or was Richard smitten? If he was, I could be in serious trouble. My defense might go right out the window. I'd never seen him show the slightest interest in any woman. Not that he was gay, he was just a confirmed bachelor, who believed that women were distractions to be kept at arm's length while in pursuit of the greater good, i.e., money. If Richard were under her spell, this woman must be something else. Which I would have noticed if I weren't in so much trouble. How attractive was she, for Pete's sake? Oh, my God, I'm staring at her breasts.

I snapped out of it in time to hear ADA Fairfield assuring Richard she was familiar with *The Godfather*.

"I'd love to discuss movie trivia with you, but we have this matter at hand. Your client claims he was rescuing a girl who had been abducted. Her parents claim he was the one doing the abducting."

"Due to a simple misunderstanding. They didn't hire him, and they have no reason to believe anyone else would. Nonetheless, it happened. And it's a good thing it did, since he did in fact rescue the girl."

"Rescue her from what?"

"It is not my place to make accusations," Richard said. "And I certainly don't want to say anything that would be actionable, but let's suppose he took her away from a grown-up who let her smoke dope and filled her full of margaritas until she couldn't be responsible for her actions. I don't expect the parents to be grateful. They're confused, they don't want to think anything bad about their daughter. But that's no reason to make my client the bad guy. I would think you'd want to take a good hard look at the guy who brought the girl to Philadelphia in the first place."

"I'd be more inclined to do that if your client were actually claiming to have *done* the things he's hypothetically suggesting. It's a little hard to whip up much interest in a what-if."

"Would you like to discuss this over dinner?"

Her eyes twinkled. "Are you hitting on me?"

"No. We're plea bargaining. I open with dinner and we cop to disorderly conduct and a five-hundred-dollar fine, you counter with drinks and endangering the welfare of a minor, six months suspended."

She smiled. "I hear you're good in court."

"Really? I'm a negligence lawyer. How would you hear that?"

"One hears stories. The Brandeis settlement, for instance."

The Brandeis settlement involved Richard getting his client a bundle of cash from the store he was in the process of robbing, even though he had been found guilty of the burglary, and was actually in jail when the civil suit came to trial.

"I'm flattered," Richard said. "But I have this client."

"Yeah. And without these allegeds and hypotheticals and what-ifs, he claims he followed the girl down to Philadelphia, where he managed to slip her chloral hydrate, wrest her away from her abductor, and bring her back to her parents. And he claims her mother hired her, only she says she didn't, and he now claims it was not her mother, but someone posing as her mother. However, he doesn't claim it was someone posing as Congressman Blake who took her, he claims it was the congressman himself."

Richard turned to me. "Stanley?"

"Are we talking hypothetically?"

"Absolutely."

"I hate to jump to conclusions, but according to his license plate number, and his photos on Facebook, that's the guy."

Richard turned to the pretty ADA. "There you are."

She frowned. For the first time since she'd come in she didn't look happy. "Give me moment. I'd like to check this out."

The minute she was gone I turned on Richard. "What the hell are you doing?"

"Excuse me?"

"I'm in trouble, and you're playing kissy face with the ADA."

"Stanley. That's a rather harsh assessment of my services. Here I am, rushing to your rescue, and no one's even dead. I thought you weren't going to call me for anything short of a murder."

"I'm sorry, but the charges were piling up. When you put rape on the table—"

"There's a nice image."

"Not what I meant, but I see the way your mind's going. Who the hell is this ADA, anyway?"

"I don't know, but she seems to have a firm grasp of the legal issues."

"She thinks I'm guilty."

Richard shrugged. "That's her only flaw. Otherwise, she's quite nice."

"Richard."

"Stanley, are you in court when I get my settlements? More to the point, are you in my settlement conferences on the cases that don't go to court? That's where I make most of my money. In simple horse trading. I'm pretty damn good."

"This isn't horse trading."

"Sure it is. No judge involved. No actual laws in play. Just a simple discussion of how best to resolve the situation."

"Richard. I've seen you in action before. You don't trade horses. You cut the other cowboy in little pieces and take his horse as a trophy. Why are you letting this woman walk all over you?"

Richard sighed. "Oh, Stanley. You have a lot to learn."

The door opened and the ADA I had a lot to learn about came back, ushering in Congressman Blake.

He leveled a finger at me, said, "Is that him? Is that the son of a bitch?"

Richard, delighted to have someone to bop around rather than the comely ADA, stepped in front of me and said, "If you would like to characterize this man in terms that are actionable, feel free, but I would like to point out unless you can *prove* he's a son of a bitch, it would be my pleasure to demonstrate for you how much cash it's worth."

The congressman was not one to back down. "Oh, yeah? Who the hell are you?"

"I'm Mr. Hastings's attorney. I don't want to tell you your business, but if you were hoping for a campaign contribution, I'd moderate your tone."

"Jokes? You're making jokes? You client kidnapped a girl, and everyone's blaming me."

"Funny about that," I said.

Richard shot me a warning look.

The attractive ADA stepped in. "Please. I'd like to clear this up, which doesn't appear to be that easy under the circumstances. It would be nice if we can get through this without recriminations."

"I'd like that," Richard said. "But I'm not offering an oral stipulation that people aren't bound by what they say."

"Wonderful," the congressman said. "After your client's already shot his mouth off."

"And that's just the type of remark we'd like to avoid," ADA Fairfield said. "Let's see if I can speed this along. Without anyone accusing anyone of anything, let's suppose Mr. Hastings here thought you'd abducted a girl."

"Ridiculous," the congressman said.

"Do you deny you took Sharon to Philadelphia?" I said.

"Stanley," Richard cautioned.

"Go on. Ask him if he denies it."

"*I'll* ask him," ADA Fairfield said. "Mr. Blake, did you take Sharon Weldon to Philadelphia?"

"Yes, I did."

I exhaled in exasperation, spread my hands. "That wasn't so hard, was it?"

"And while you were there, did you smoke dope with her and buy her alcoholic beverages?"

"Absolutely not."

"Did you take her backstage at the Show Palace where they were smoking dope?"

"I'm a congressman, not a cop. It's not my job to police drug use at music events."

"It is when you take a minor."

"Stanley! Do I have to tie and gag you?"

"I can assure you she didn't smoke dope."

"He bought her margaritas," I persisted.

Richard sighed, shook his head. "My client is an idiot. I think we can all agree on that. But he's not a liar. If he says he saw Congressman Blake buy her margaritas, I would trust his word."

"Did you buy her margaritas?" ADA Fairfield asked.

He smiled. "*Virgin* margaritas. No alcohol. They look just the same. Even have salt on the rim."

"Well, you had that one ready," I said.

This time is was ADA Fairfield who gave me the disparaging look.

"Why are you quibbling over details?" I said. "The fact is, the guy took her to Philadelphia."

"And why'd you do that, Mr. Blake?"

"To see my son, Adam. Sharon's a friend of his. She's never seen him perform. Adam's a singer. In a boy band. They're the opening act this week."

I stared at him. "What?"

"Her parents knew she was going. That's why they were so upset I lost her. I don't blame them. If someone abducted Adam, I'd go crazy."

My head spun as layers and layers of misconceptions peeled off of me. The fact that they were steeped in perfidy didn't help. It was somewhat overwhelming. "Adam is one of those god-awful singers?" I said incredulously.

"What my client means to say," Richard put in hastily, "is that he is surprised to discover that one of the talented young men gracing the stage at last night's entertainment was your son, and he is certainly sorry if he inconvenienced you in any way." He raised an eyebrow at the attractive ADA. "Sharon's parents will confirm this story?"

"They already have."

"Really?" Richard cocked his head, side-spied at her narrowly. "So. You *knew* all this. But you didn't let on. You brought the congressman in here and made my client jump through hoops anyway."

She stuck out her chin. "So?"

Richard smiled. "I *like* that."

20

ALICE WAS SUPPORTIVE. IN HER FASHION. HER FASHION IS irony and gentle ridicule. I've gotten used to it over the years. Even so.

"You were duped?" Alice said. "By a woman?"

"Yes."

"An attractive woman?"

"That's neither here nor there."

"*She's* neither here nor there. Isn't that right? She's totally disappeared?"

"Yes, she has."

"Of course, she didn't really exist. That makes it easier, doesn't it? To vanish, I mean. She has no obligations to fulfill. If she were someone, you could say, well, she's gotta get her car registered, her teeth fixed, her hair done, and check those places out. But that's not the case. She's elusive as air. No strings. No ties. No name. No face."

"I saw her face."

"But you don't have her picture. And with your knack for description, she might as well have been wearing a paper bag. I remember what you did with a sketch artist once."

"There's no reason to snipe."

"I wasn't sniping. Just pointing out the facts."

Which was true. Alice is very good at finding facts that snipe.

"So," Alice said, "we have a mystery woman, and all we know is that she duped you."

"She had blonde hair."

"Which could be a wig. It probably was, if she was assuming a false identity. Did she have nice tits?"

"Didn't notice."

"I'll take that as a yes. It would have to be, or you wouldn't have been duped."

"That's silly."

"I know, but you're like that. If she didn't have nice tits you'd have been skeptical. Found reason to doubt her story."

"That's stupid."

"I know, but I married you anyway."

"Come on, Alice. This wasn't my fault. I was told a plausible lie to arouse my sympathy."

"Oh, that's what she aroused."

"That's feeble, Alice."

"Sorry. Couldn't resist."

"Actually, I set you up for it."

"I know."

We lay there in companionable silence. Or what I chose to consider companionable silence. Alice might have considered it something else. The silent treatment, for instance.

Alice broke it first. "So, the case is over?"

"Huh?"

"You've been paid, right?"

"Ah. Yeah."

"You hesitate?"

"I had some expenses."

"Oh, God."

"It's not like that."

"What's it like?"

"Well, two hundred dollars for chloral hydrate. Two fifty for Amtrak tickets. A hundred-dollar cover charge at the nightclub. Plus taxi cabs and bribes."

"What does that come to?"

"About six hundred dollars."

"So, you broke even."

"Yeah."

Alice nodded encouragingly. "You're getting better."

21

MacAullif was more straightforward. "So, you fucked up."

"I had a reversal of fortune."

He burst out laughing. "Well, that's one way to put it. But basically, you screwed the pooch."

"I was set up and lied to."

"Hard to believe anyone could do that."

"*You* thought the woman was legit."

"I never met the woman. I was going on what you told me."

"You traced the license plate for me."

"I see. It's my fault. If I hadn't given you the name of the congressman, this never would have happened. I'll remember to point that out the next time you ask for a favor."

"So, what do I do now?"

"What do you do now? I don't know what you do now. I know what you *don't* do now. You don't hassle the congressman anymore.

You don't hassle the girl, and you don't hassle her parents. You stay as far the fuck away from every last one of them as you possibly can. And for the next few weeks you have your wife open the front door, in case it might be a process server filing papers on behalf of someone who might want to sue you. And I imagine there might be a line."

"Yeah, but—"

"But what?"

"How do I find out what happened?"

MacAullif looked at me as if I'd just won Moron of the Month. "Who *gives* a shit what happened? You don't *have* to know what happened. No one's *paying* you to find *out* what happened. What happened is, someone went to a lot of trouble to make you look stupid. Which shows they're not very bright. It doesn't *take* much to make you look stupid. Why bother with all the window dressing?"

"That's what I'd like to find out."

"But you're not *going* to. You're going to poke around where you got no business and get yourself in *more* trouble. When you do, don't expect me to get you out."

"I have an attorney."

"I know. He called me. Said if I heard from you, to pass along a message. 'Nothing short of murder.' You know what that means?"

"I have an idea."

"So, it might not be a good time for you to get arrested for something stupid. Like poking around the congressman, for instance."

"I bet he's dirty."

"That may well be. But I bet his story checks out."

"Oh."

"Why do you say that?"

"My wife Googled him."

"I'm sorry."

"Don't be an asshole. She checked him out on the computer. His son is in a boy band performing in Philadelphia. Which should be a crime in itself."

"So, you're going to leave him alone."

I waggled my hand. "Well . . ."

"Oh, for Christ's sake."

MacAullif took a cigar out of his desk drawer, always a bad sign. His doctor had made him give up cigars, but he played with them when I annoyed him. He played with them a lot. "Let me give you some advice. Take some time off. Go to the country. Go to the beach. Go to Mexico."

"Mexico? Why Mexico?"

"It's not *here*. You need to lie low, recharge your batteries, give those around you a break." MacAullif waggled the cigar. "Just a hint."

"And I appreciate it. I just don't have time right now."

He squinted at me suspiciously. "Why not? More to the point, why are you *here*?"

"I'm wondering what type of stuff the congressman might be into. The type of stuff *not* on Google."

MacAullif stared at me openmouthed. "Are you an idiot?"

"MacAullif."

"No, no, no. I talk, you listen, but nothing gets through. We have an entire conversation at the end of which you act like we didn't. Like nothing was said. You're like a kid listening to his parent You nod yes and ignore everything."

"You're missing the point."

MacAullif gripped the cigar as if it were a baseball bat. If it had been, I think he would have bashed my head in. "*I'm* missing the point? You think *I'm* missing the point?"

"About the congressman," I explained patiently. "I'll tell you why."

"Not if I throw you out on your ear."

"Not worth it," I said. "It will make a big fuss, and all day people will be asking you why you did it. Or I can give you my spiel in two minutes and walk out."

MacAullif took a huge breath. Calmed himself. Raised a finger. "*One* minute," he said, and sat back down.

"Okay. Someone went to a great deal of trouble to make me look stupid. For no discernable reason. On the other hand, they made the congressman look stupid. Worse, to look like a child molester. Granted, it was totally unconvincing, and easily explained away. But the guy's in politics. Facts don't mean that much to politicians. They can smear each other with just a hint of a scandal. So, I have to ask myself, is the congressman involved in anything that anyone might want to influence, and/or throw a monkey wrench into by putting him in an embarrassing position?" I looked at my watch. "Done!"

MacAullif scowled, exhaled. Gnawed on his cigar. He didn't look at all happy.

But he didn't throw me out the door.

22

"You've got a lot of nerve."

"I made a mistake and I'm sorry."

"You drugged my daughter."

"I made a mistake."

"Drugging a young girl isn't a mistake. It's a criminal act. My God!"

Sharon's mom looked good. Sharon's real mom, who was pissed at me, not Sharon's fake mom, who played me for a sucker. It occurred to me, I was not having much luck with Sharon's moms, real or imaginary. But Jennifer Weldon was looking rather hot in a sleeveless yellow pullover and tennis shorts. I don't know how I'd ever mistaken her for a cop. Not that women cops aren't good looking. I'm sure some are. And not just the ones on TV, either. Did that sound condescending? It did, didn't it. Good God, why do I always get in trouble with women?

I was in Sharon's mom's apartment. The one where Sharon lived with her actual mom, and not with Sharon's fake mom, who also claimed to live there. I'd talked my way past the doorman, who wasn't going to let me in, and had rung upstairs to confirm the fact that Mrs. Weldon didn't want to see me. She'd let me in, if only to bawl me out. Or perhaps stupefied by the fact I actually wished to see her.

"I thought your daughter was in danger. I thought I was acting in her best interests."

"How could you think that? Are you a moron?"

"Yes, I am. But I had help. A woman posing as you hired me to do it."

"Hired you to drug my daughter?"

"No."

"Well, which is it? Were you hired to do it or weren't you?"

"I was hired to get your daughter away from the congressman and bring her home."

"This woman knew Sharon was with the congressman?"

"Ah . . . I don't know."

"What do you mean, you don't know? She either asked you to get her away from the congressman or she didn't."

"She asked me to get her away from a man. I don't know if she knew the man was the congressman."

"You mean she never said so."

"Ah . . ."

"What's the problem? Either she said so or she didn't."

"Well, she did, but I don't know if she knew."

"That makes no sense. What do you mean?"

"Well, *I* told *her* he was the congressman. But I have no way of knowing whether she knew he was the congressman before I told her."

"Oh, for goodness sakes."

Jennifer Weldon sank down on her rather nicely upholstered couch in her rather expensively furnished living room. I could either sit down myself, which would be presumptuous, or remain standing, from which position I could see down her shirt.

Her eyes flashed. "Why are you here? What is it you want?"

"I'm not happy with the situation. And I don't mean mine. I'm not here to get you to drop the charges."

"You want me to drop the charges?"

"I just said I didn't." I sighed. "That's a lie. Of course I want you to drop the charges. But that's not why I'm here, and it's not what I'm asking. I'm here because I don't like being played for a sucker. And I'm sure you don't, either. Even if you didn't know it. This woman claimed to be you. I don't know why, but you put your finger right on it, asking about the congressman. I don't know if she knew the congressman, but my hunch is she did. My hunch is that's *why* she did what she did. So, I'm wondering if *you* knew the congressman."

"What are you implying?"

"I'm not implying anything. I'm trying to make sense of a situation that doesn't. There has to be a reason I was duped into doing the things I did. I'm wondering if anyone has a reason to embarrass the congressman. He has a wife and kid. Probably couldn't afford to be caught in a sexual scandal."

"There's nothing between me and Jason Blake."

"I never said there was. I'm talking about the scandal with your daughter."

"There's no scandal with my daughter."

"I know. But this person tried to manufacture one. If that was done to embarrass the congressman, why would anyone want to?"

"I have no idea."

"Did he have any project coming up this might impact?"

"I know nothing about his political life."

"Just his personal life?"

"No, not his personal life. There's nothing about his personal life that would interest anyone. Perfectly ordinary family man. Wife and kid. Stable marriage."

"Are you sure about that?"

"Yes, I am. We know them socially. Our daughter is friends with their son. They've dined here. Valerie's a gem."

"That's his wife?"

"That's right. And I don't think she'd take kindly to your insinuations."

"Would she take kindly to me trying to find out who's setting up her husband?"

"Is that what you're doing?"

"It's the only way to clear myself. Look. I'm not the world's best private eye, but I fight for my clients. A woman hired me, and I tried to do what she wanted. That screwed everything up, and I'd like to make it right."

"Oh, you're just a do-gooder."

"I already said I wasn't. I'm tired of justifying myself. I've apologized. I've explained. I've told you my intentions. I mean to get to the bottom of this. You know anything that might help I'd be glad to hear it. Otherwise, I'll go it on my own."

I turned started for the door.

"Wait."

I turned back.

She got up from the couch, came toward me. "What do you want to know?"

"I was told Sharon was having a sleepover with a friend. That if she did, I could go home. I was told that's what you'd been told. That Sharon had told her parents she was having a sleepover. The mother believed that was just a cover story to get out of the house. I was told that to alert me to the fact that anything Sharon did *other* than go home to a friend's house was something illicit I should put a stop to."

"Yeah. So?"

"Was that a likely lie? I mean, I know nothing about her, so I'd buy it. But for someone who knew Sharon, was that something she would normally do? Not lie about a sleepover and run off to Philadelphia. Have a sleepover to begin with. I mean, in the normal course of events would she have a sleepover with a girlfriend?"

"Yes. She's done it several times."

"So. This woman seemed to know your business. You sure that wasn't you in a wig?"

"Now, see here."

"No, no, I know it wasn't. I'm just saying, whoever pulled this off had all the facts and did it well. It was obviously someone who knew about Sharon's relationship with the congressman's kid, and knew the congressman would fall right into the trap."

"You mean *you* would."

"Yes. I would. But I wasn't the principal. No one gave a damn about me."

"Now you're feeling slighted?"

I grimaced, but that was actually a victory. The woman was joking with me, at my expense. She'd become, like Alice, Richard, and MacAullif, one of the people picking on me. In the realm of my existence, that made her a friend.

Having scored with sarcasm, Mom went on the attack. "This mystery woman. We have only your word she actually exists."

"Oh, she exists, all right. She's most likely an actress, fed the information, hired to do a job."

"What makes you think that?"

"Because that's usually the case."

"Usually? This has happened to you before? That you've been duped by an actress hired to play a part?"

I had, actually. Not that it had anything to do with the present situation. It occurred to me I would do well to keep my mouth shut. "You're missing the point. The point is, whoever did this had inside information. If they're familiar with the parties involved, they probably know them personally. In which case, they need to keep a low profile. If you were behind this, for instance, you wouldn't come into my office and ask me to follow your daughter. You'd hire an actress and prime her to do so."

"Are you serious?"

"Not about you doing it. But about the way it would need to be done. Now, setting everything aside, can you think of anyone who would want to harm the congressman?"

"Absolutely not."

I shook my head.

"Too bad."

23

NEXT ORDER OF BUSINESS WAS THE CONGRESSMAN HIMSELF. Unfortunately, he wouldn't see me, and there was no way I was getting by *his* doorman. The son of a bitch knew me from my abortive attempt to get a look at the parking garage security tapes.

On the other hand, the guy couldn't work all the time. He'd have shifts. All I had to do was find the right shift.

I drove over to the East Side, got a meter on Madison, walked over and checked out his building from across the street.

There was a different doorman on duty.

Excellent.

Now all I needed was the congressman to be home. I had done my research in that department. When Congress wasn't in session, he often hung out in his apartment. His son was in school. His wife worked. Anyone there would be him.

Unfortunately, his number was unlisted.

I whipped out my cell phone, called MacAullif.

He wasn't pleased to hear from me. And he was less pleased when he heard why I was calling.

"You want the congressman's phone number?"

"Well, I know you don't want me to apologize in person. But the man must feel wronged."

"Didn't I give you his number?"

"You gave me his address."

"And it's too much trouble to look it up."

"It's unlisted."

"If I give you the number, you gonna blame me for it when you go to jail?"

"Absolutely not."

"Even if I tip him off to trace the call?"

"That sounds a little hostile, MacAullif."

He gave me the number to get me off the phone.

I punched it in, hit SEND.

I got a busy signal.

Great. He was home. But he'd never let me by the front desk. I needed to get upstairs and ring his doorbell.

I called Alice. "Can you get me the number of a tenant at 521 Fifth Avenue."

"Which tenant?"

"I don't care."

"Stanley."

"All right. A female tenant. Get me a woman who lives there."

"What the hell are you doing?"

"I'm trying to stay out of trouble."

"And this will help you?"

"You have no idea."

"Hang on."

Alice set down the phone. I could hear her typing into the computer.

It took her thirty seconds. "Mildred Finnegan."

"How'd you get that?"

"I Googled the address and searched for news articles. A Mildred Finnegan at that address took second place at some bake fair."

"Terrific. You're sure she lives there?"

"Absolutely. I cross-checked it. Once I got the name, I looked it up and came up with the listing."

"Great. You got the phone number?"

"Sure."

Alice gave me the number, and I wrote it down.

I hung up with Alice, called the number she gave me. A woman answered and I hung up.

I went over to Madison Avenue, found a flower shop.

"I want to send some flowers."

"What kind?"

"The kind that look pretty and smell good. I don't know. A bunch of cut flowers. Can you help me out?"

"Sure."

The guy looked like he owned the shop, a little old man with avaricious eyes. I could see him calculating the minute I left it up to him.

"Something in the neighborhood of twenty bucks," I told him.

That dampened his spirits considerably. "Including delivery?"

"No. For the bouquet."

"Great."

He grabbed some wrapping papers, picked out a selection of pretty but no doubt inexpensive flowers, added a few greens. "How's that?"

"What's that going to run me?"

"Thirty bucks."

So. Ten bucks for delivery. Seeing as how it was right around the corner, that was a nice bonus.

I handed him the page from my notebook on which I'd written Mildred Finnegan's name and address.

The florist wrote up the delivery slip, attached it to the bouquet.

"When will this go out?"

"Soon as my boy gets back."

"When's that?"

"Shouldn't be long."

"On second thought," I said, "maybe I'll drop 'em off myself."

His face hardened. "You wanted delivery. Our price was fixed on delivery."

"Hey, don't sweat it. I'll pay you for delivery. Here's thirty bucks. I just want it to go out now. I'll drop it with the doorman myself, you don't have to send your boy, everybody's happy."

"Fine."

"You got a card?"

"Sure."

He gave me a little card in an envelope. I think he considered charging me, and thought better of it. I took a pen, wrote, "For Mildred," on the envelope. On the card I wrote "XXX." I signed it, "You know who." I put the card in the envelope and sealed it.

I took the flowers back to the congressman's apartment building.

"I have a delivery for Mildred Finnegan," I told the doorman.

"You can leave it with me."

"I was told to hand deliver."

"I can sign for it."

"Yeah. They said to give it to her personally."

"There's no reason for that."

"There is for me. Could you call up and ask her?"

The doorman figured I was hoping for a tip. He smirked, but he made the call. "Mrs. Finnegan, I have some flowers here for you. Can the delivery boy bring them up?" He listened, covered the phone. "Who are they from?"

"I don't know." I raised my voice. "There's a card. You want me to take it out and read it?"

The telephone made squawking noises.

"Yes, yes, of course, Mrs. Finnegan." The doorman hung up the phone. "You can go on up."

"What apartment?"

"8A."

Mrs. Finnegan gave me a two-dollar tip.

I felt good I was finally making money on this case until I remembered the flowers had set me back thirty bucks.

No mind. I walked right by the elevator, ducked into the stairwell, climbed the flights to the congressman's floor

I walked down the hall and rang his bell.

There was no answer.

I waited a while, rang again.

Nothing.

I put my head to the door and listened.

It gave. Thank God I wasn't really leaning on it or I'd have been flat on the floor. I caught my balance and straightened up as the door swung open.

This was not good. This was never good. I've read hundreds of mysteries, and when the door swings open there's always a dead body on the other side.

I knew that couldn't be in this case, the congressman was there, the congressman was alive, I'd called and his phone was busy. So there had to be another explanation. He was expecting someone so he left the door open. He hadn't answered the bell because he was in the john. Or he was in the bedroom with the TV on loud and couldn't hear it. Or he was on the phone and couldn't come to the door. Or maybe he didn't mean to leave the door open, he just didn't shut it all the way, that happens to me a lot in my apartment, the little whoozit doesn't engage and it's still open.

For whatever reason, I'd just solved my number one problem. How I was going to get in the door.

I pushed the door open and walked in, then closed, but didn't latch it behind me, in case he had left it open for someone.

I found myself in a rather sumptuous foyer with a bench, an umbrella stand, a coatrack, and two closet doors. There was a painting on the wall in front of me, though whether real or a copy I couldn't say. I tiptoed in, poked my head around the corner.

Inside was a spacious living room, with couches, coffee tables, a bar, and a grand piano.

"Mr. Blake?" I called. "Congressman?"

There was no answer.

I walked into the room and stopped dead.

There was a fireplace against the side wall. The congressman lay on the hearth. A poker from the fireplace lay next to him.

If it didn't match the gash in the back of his head, I'd have been quite surprised.

24

OH, MY GOD.

All my worst fears realized. Here's the dead body I was worried about. It happens to be the one person who could have helped me, but that's rather minor now.

Okay, so what could I do? I knew I should call the police, but what would I tell 'em? I was in a very embarrassing position, having tricked my way into the building. It wouldn't take much to make me the number one suspect. Throw in my history with the congressman and I'd look good, even to me.

So, what if I ran? Hightailed it the hell out of there? It would be a while before the body was found. By then I'd be long gone. True, if the cops picked me up and showed me to the doorman, I'd be dead meat, but why would they do that?

Because he'd tell them about the delivery man.

No, he wouldn't. The delivery wasn't to the congressman. It was to Mrs. Finnegan. Why the hell would he even think of it? He sent a delivery man up to Mrs. Finnegan. The delivery man went up to Mrs. Finnegan. She got her flowers, I got my tip. All I had to do was walk through the lobby folding the bills and putting them in my pocket, and the doorman would smirk and forget me. By the time the body was found there wouldn't be any reason to remember a routine flower delivery to another apartment.

Unless the cops connected me with the congressman from the nightclub, and checked up just in case. But would they put me in a lineup for the doorman just on the off chance? Why should they? No one came to see the congressman.

Except the person who killed him. The doorman would be bound to mention them.

But only if the cops knew the time of death. Well, not only, but much more likely. If the cops knew when he died, the person who was with him then would be in the soup.

If they didn't, whoever found the body could get blamed. Which would totally screw things up. Even if the cops knew that person didn't do it, whoever found the body would be a whacking good reasonable doubt for the defense attorney to throw at the jury once the cops charged the real killer. Could you say *the real killer* these days? Has it been enough time? Or would folks still think of O.J.?

Jesus Christ, should I call the cops?

It occurred to me that as long as I was doing my Hamlet impression—to flee, or not to flee—I might as well do something useful.

I searched the body.

The congressman was wearing a lightweight sports jacket. I checked the pockets. I don't know what I was looking for. Maybe a list of names conveniently titled: CAMPAIGN CONTRIBU-TORS. There was no such list.

I took out the congressman's wallet. Inside were his driver's license, registration, credit cards, and two hundred and sixty-two dollars in cash. I didn't steal it. I stuck the wallet back in the congressman's hip pocket.

It was all wrong. This was the part where the private eye was supposed to find a clue that didn't mean anything now but would eventually tie in with something completely unrelated and lead to unmasking the killer.

I found diddly-squat.

I'd been stupid long enough. It was time for option B. Which was stupider still.

I stood up, yanked the handkerchief out of my pocket, polished anything I might have touched, from the wallet to the knob on the front door. I closed it behind me but left the latch unengaged, just the way I'd found it.

I slipped into the stairwell, went down to 8, in case the doorman watched what floors the elevator stopped on. Hoped he wouldn't notice how long I'd been there.

He did.

As I came through the lobby, making a show of shoving the tip in my pocket, he gave me more than a casual smirk. I was so rattled that it took me a moment to get it. He figured I'd had a matinee with Mrs. Finnegan. I felt bad if I'd sullied her reputation. I wondered if I should send her some flowers.

The doorman seemed inclined to chat. Luckily, a guy came in just then, and I slipped away while the doorman dealt with him.

I went out to the street, hunted up a pay phone. Not as easy as it used to be. Now that everyone has a cell phone, who needs 'em? I had to walk four blocks to find one that worked.

I dropped in a quarter, called 911.

The phone asked for fifty cents.

I cursed it, dug in my pocket for another quarter.

At least they answered right away. "What is your emergency?"

"I want to report a break-in at 521 Fifth Avenue, apartment 12B. The intruder was armed, and there may be injuries."

"And who are you?"

I hung up, went back to my car.

The meter had run out, but I hadn't gotten a ticket. Small consolation. I'd still blown thirty bucks for flowers.

That and finding a dead body made it a pretty bad day.

25

WENDY WAS SURPRISED TO SEE ME. THAT'S RICHARD'S secretary, Wendy, one half of the Wendy/Janet team. I can tell 'em apart in person. In fact, they don't look at all alike. It's just their voices I can't distinguish.

"What are you doing here?" Wendy said. "I thought you were off the clock."

"I am."

"I don't understand. Haven't you turned in all your cases?"

"Yes."

"And we mail you your checks."

"I came to see Richard."

"He's rather busy. Preparing for court."

"Just tell him I'm here."

"I hate to disturb him."

"I'll make sure he knows it wasn't your fault."

"How you gonna do that if he won't see you?"

Wendy/Janet had the IQ of a badly pruned parsnip, but it was all directed toward self-preservation. If either of them expended as much energy toward doing their jobs as they did toward trying to keep them, they'd be ten times as competent.

"Fine. Don't tell Richard I want to see him. Just give him a message. Tell him MacAullif gave me *his* message, and I'm complying with it to the letter."

She sighed, picked up the phone, relayed my message.

Moments later, Richard flung open the door. "Stanley. Are you serious?"

"Absolutely."

"You're not just yanking my chain?"

"Would I do that?"

"Or pissing me off with some technically correct interpretation of what I said?"

I shook my head. "Nope. It's the real deal."

"Come in."

Richard ushered me into his inner office, shut the door on Wendy's eavesdropping ears.

I brought him up to speed on the congressman's demise.

Richard was incredulous. "You found the body and left it?"

"If I'd reported it, I'd be calling you from the police station."

"Yeah, but the charges would be less. We wouldn't have compounding a felony and conspiring to conceal a crime."

"We'd still have murder," I pointed out.

"Yeah, but I can probably get you off on murder. The other charges are more difficult, since you're actually guilty."

"That's a rather negative attitude, Richard."

"So, why are you here? I said murder, not obstruction of justice."

"It's a murder."

"You're not accused of it."

"Well, I will be, if the police find out. Isn't that good enough?"

"No. It's absolutely horrible. You left the scene of the crime.

Flight is an indication of guilt. I don't want a murder case I can't win. Where's the fun in that?"

"You're giving up? You can't get me off? You want me to hire another lawyer?"

"Another lawyer won't work for you. Lawyers have licenses. Some of them have ethics. None of them wants to mess with the Bar Association. Which is where a lawyer for you is apt to wind up. I'm the only one stupid enough to mess around with you, and that's just because I'm such a softie."

"I know, I know. You're a prince. So what do I do?"

"All right. How bad is it? Let's see. The doorman can identify you as going into the building, but not to that floor. Did he have any reason to remember you particularly?"

"He thought I was shtupping Mrs. Finnegan."

"The doorman's Jewish?"

"He's Hispanic."

"And he thought you were doing the tenant? Okay, that's a reason to remember you. When they can't find anyone else who went to the apartment, they'll come up with that."

"But they have to find someone who went to that apartment."
"Why?"

"Because someone killed him."

"You mean besides you."

"I didn't kill him."

"I never thought you did. The police may feel differently."

"That doesn't mean they'll stop looking for someone else."

"I suppose," Richard said.

"You're not convinced."

"Well, think about it. If the cops pick you for this, it's because they got a lead from the doorman. If the doorman fingers you as going up, it's because he couldn't name anybody else. Because anybody *known* to be going to the congressman's apartment would be such a better suspect, they wouldn't even be looking for you."

I frowned.

"That doesn't make sense?"

"No. It does."

"You better pray the cops solve this damn thing. That's your only hope now. That the police figure out who did it before they decide it's you."

"And if they don't?"

"Then *you* better figure out who did it."

"How the hell do I do that?"

"Oh, I don't know. I'm just the lawyer on the case. You're the detective."

"Basically, you'd like me to solve the case so you don't have to do any work."

"My inclination to work is directly proportional to the size of the retainer. How much are you paying me, again?"

"Never mind." I shook my head. "So, as my attorney, would you advise me to turn myself in?"

"Not unless you have a death wish."

The phone rang.

Richard scooped it up. "Not now, Wendy. Hold my calls." Which should have done it. Wendy doesn't argue with Richard. Only this time he said, "What? . . . Really? . . . Okay, I'll tell him."

Richard hung up the phone. "You can forget what I said about contacting the cops."

"Oh? Why?"

"MacAullif wants to see you."

26

MacAullif took out a cigar. After a moment, he took out another. He left them on the desk, prominently displayed in an ominous position. He looked at me, cocked his head. "So?"

"So, what?"

"Anything you want to tell me?"

"It's your party, MacAullif. You tell me."

MacAullif picked up one of the cigars. "That phone number I gave you."

"What about it?"

"Was that any use to you?"

"Yes. I was gonna thank you. You didn't have to drag me in here."

"So it *was* of use. Just *how* was it of use?"

"Why do you ask?"

"I was hoping to get an answer. I *intend* to get an answer. If I *don't* get an answer, it will not be pleasant."

"Well, we wouldn't want that. You gave me the number, I called the congressman."

"What did he say?"

"Nothing. I got a busy signal."

"Your call never went through?"

"That's right."

"You didn't call him back?"

"No."

"Why not?"

"I couldn't think of anything I wanted to say."

"Then why did you call him in the first place?"

"It would have been inconsiderate not to after you went and looked up the number."

MacAullif twirled the cigar between his fingers like a baton. He wasn't good at it. You'd think after years of trying he'd be better.

"You see what's happening here?" MacAullif said. "I'm giving you an opportunity to volunteer information. You're not doing it. This is using up a great deal of your credibility with the police in general and me in particular."

"I got all that. Even without your explanation."

"So, you got anything you want to tell me?"

"Not particularly."

"Too bad. Guess who's dead."

"The congressman?"

"Now how do you know that?"

"Why would you care if it was anyone else?"

"So that was a wild guess?"

"Not so wild, if I'm right. How'd he die?"

"Wanna take a wild guess at that?"

"I'd rather hear it from you."

"I'll bet you would. He was whacked over the head with a poker. Bashed in his skull. Died almost instantly. Fell in the hearth."

"In the hearth?"

"Yeah."

"Any chance he just tripped and hit his head?"

"The back of his head with the front of the poker?" MacAullif scowled. "That's not as stupid as it sounds. The body was face down. The back of his head was up. His face was covered with ashes. The back of his head was not. He had fallen face down in the hearth after being hit in the back of the head while standing up. The murder weapon was lying next to the body."

"You search it for prints?"

"I'm sure you wiped yours off."

"I didn't kill him, MacAullif."

"I never thought you did. Not really your style. Of course, I know you. Other cops may take a less generous view."

"I'm sure you'll straighten them out."

MacAullif ignored that, picked up the second cigar. "You know how the cops found the body?"

"You said face down in the hearth."

"That's *where* they found the body. I mean what led them to it. They got an anonymous tip."

"Oh?"

"Pay phone on Madison Avenue. Four blocks from the apartment. Just where the killer would call from, if he wanted to leave an anonymous tip."

"Why would a killer do that?"

"I have no idea. On the other hand, if a wiseass private eye stumbled over the body, that's the phone he would probably use. It's the closest working pay phone to the crime scene. So if a private eye wanted to report the crime, but knew his cell phone would be traced . . ."

"If a private eye did that, would it be a crime?"

"Finding a dead body and failing to report it? Sure it would be a crime."

"That's not failing to report it. That's reporting it."

"Failing to report it in a timely fashion."

"What's a timely fashion? Ten minutes? Fifteen minutes? I'd like to see a lawyer have a go at that one."

"I hope it doesn't come to that."

"Me, too. Be a huge waste of time."

"Which brings us back to the phone number I gave you. It's a big problem for me. If you took that phone number I gave you, used it to see if the congressman was at home, somehow got in to see him, found him dead, hightailed it out of there and made an anonymous phone call to the police to tip them off, it would put me in very bad position. I would be obliged to turn you in. Otherwise, I could be suspended. Possibly lose my pension." MacAullif sighed. "You see the position I'm in?"

He looked truly distraught.

"What do you want me to do?"

MacAullif's lip quivered.

Oh, my God! He was going to cry. This macho, tough, beefy cop was actually going to cry. It was an amazing, extraordinary human moment.

I didn't want to see it.I didn't want to be a part of it. I didn't want to humiliate MacAullif in a manner that would haunt our relationship, if any, for years to come.

His lip quivered some more. His face twisted, and . . .

He burst out laughing.

There he was, rocking up and down in his chair, roaring with laughter, pointing the cigars at me. "Gotcha, didn't I? I really had you going! Oh, if you could see the look on your face. It was priceless. Poor fuck wondering what the hell you were going to do."

I blinked. "MacAullif?"

"I swear to God," MAcAullif said between guffaws, "for a minute I thought you were going to cop to the thing. You were really buying it."

I blinked again. "And just what was I buying?"

"The whole found-the-body bit. I could see the scenario playing out in your head. Suppose you copped to finding the body and making the phone call, even though it wasn't true, just to cut me a break. Would the cops take that at face value? Or would they peg you for the crime? I mean, I could see you in your super do-gooder mode, confessing to a technical offense to help me out, but copping to a felony is a bit much. Were you really going to do it?"

"Do what? MacAullif, you wanna let me in on the joke?"

"I been yanking your chain. Ever since I dragged you in here. I happen to *know* you didn't do it."

"How do you know that?"

"Cops got the killer."

I stared at him. "What?"

"Oh? Did I leave that part out? I suppose it's worth mentioning. The cops apprehended the killer at the scene of the crime. Which is a bit of a break. But what with the phone call about the disturbance and all, the cops were on the scene before the guy got away. So, while this case has every element of one I should be busting your chops for, it turns out you're in the clear."

"Oh, my God."

MacAullif nodded. "I find it had to believe myself. But that's the situation. Much as this looks like your handiwork, it isn't. Any relationship you had with the congressman is entirely coincidental, and not to be inferred."

"Who's the killer?"

"Some low-level building contractor, been making quote unquote *campaign contributions* to the congressman for a long time, evidently not happy about the congressman failing to deliver on some zoning ordinance or other. As if these things were bought and sold. 'Hey, why they hassling me? I thought I paid that off.' The congressman doesn't give him satisfaction, and the guy bashes in his head."

"Oh, my God. You say the cops found him at the crime scene?"

"That's right. Very nice. Isn't often you get one all tied up in ribbons for you."

"Got his rap sheet?"

"Didn't have one. This isn't *The Sopranos*, where a contractor is having people whacked on the side. The congressman would appear to be his first kill. And his first conviction, unless some punk ADA blows it."

"What about his record on this arrest?"

"What about it?"

"Can I see it?"

"Why?"

"I'd like to see his mug shot."

"Why?"

I wasn't sure. My head was spinning with each new bit of information. But, if what MacAullif said was true, it opened up an alarming new possibility. The killer had been there, hiding in the congressman's apartment, while I searched the body. Never mind the fact I might have been killed; in fact, it was probably a miracle I wasn't. But where was he hiding? In another room? In a closet? Was he peeking out? Did he see me? Did he see what I was doing? Did he see my face? If the killer's lawyer got him out on bail, was he someone I would have to look out for?

Might he suspect that I had spotted him?

MacAullif was back in minutes with a manila folder. He didn't hand it to me right away but went and sat behind his desk. "Now," he said, "I want you to know why I'm giving you this. I'm giving you this because you were a good boy and didn't fuck me up over the congressman's phone number. Which would be your normal course of action. I'm giving you this as an incentive to continue to strive in that direction. Am I getting through to you? Are my words having any effect?"

"I am Pavlov's dog, associating good behavior with a reward."

"Wasn't there a bell involved?" MacAullif said.

"You're so much better-educated than you act."

"Fuck you."

MacAullif handed over the file.

I flipped it open, looked at the mug shot.

I felt like I'd been slugged in the stomach.

It was the guy I'd seen in the lobby of the congressman's apartment building, coming in as I was going out.

27

I LOOKED UP TO FIND MACAULLIF WATCHING ME NARROWLY.

"Know him?" MacAullif said.

I looked at the name on the file. "Leslie Hanson? I can't say as I do."

"You looked like the mug shot surprised you."

"Well, it did. It was supposed to be a mug shot. The guy looks like a schoolteacher."

"I'm sure they kill people, too. So, there's your killer. It will be on the evening news, but you get it early for being a good boy. Now, run along. I got work to do."

This was bad. Real bad. Leslie Hanson didn't kill the congressman. I knew that. Knew it for sure. When Leslie Hanson went in, the congressman was already dead. I was the perfect alibi witness. All I had to do was open my mouth, and the guy was off the hook.

And I was on it.

What a fucking mess.

"Hang on, MacAullif. Let me think this through."

"What's to think through? Case is solved."

"Yes, but."

"But what?"

"It's a little too pat, isn't it?"

"Catching the killer does take the fun out of it," MacAullif said ironically. "But they can't all be ready for prime-time television. In real life, you have to take what you get."

"Maybe so, but tell me this? How do you know he didn't just walk in and find the guy dead."

"Couldn't happen."

"Why not?"

"Got a witness."

"Who?"

"Doorman."

"What?"

"The doorman confirms Leslie Hanson went up to see the congressman. The cops got video from the surveillance camera of the congressman's car driving into the garage. From the time he got home, the only person who came to call on him was Leslie Hanson."

"Yes, but that's not definitive."

"It's pretty damning. It's hard to kill a guy if you aren't there. The guy who *is* there is head and shoulders above a guy who isn't there on the suspect list."

"I don't see why. If you were going to kill a guy, you'd want to make damn sure you weren't identified as the guy who *was* there."

"Maybe he didn't intend to kill him. Maybe he just happened to pick up the poker."

"You're arguing against premeditation? I don't think the prosecutor's gonna like that."

"I'm only arguing with *you*. I don't think the prosecutor gives a shit about that."

"I still say it's highly likely the guy just walked in and found him."

"Then how'd he get in the door?"

"Killer left it unlocked."

"Yeah, right," MacAullif scoffed.

"Not an unlikely scenario. The killer'd *want* some scapegoat to get caught with the body."

"Sure, sure," MacAullif said. "I just let you rattle on to see how far you'd take this. But, frankly, it's getting boring. The fact is, it couldn't have happened."

"Why not?"

"I told you. We got a witness. Doorman called upstairs to tell the congressman he had a visitor. Congressman said send him up. Which more or less cinches it. Narrows the window of opportunity for your other killer from an hour and whatever down to zero. Leslie Hanson's the guy."

My head was coming off. "Wait a minute. Wait a minute. That can't be right."

"Why not? Would you rather it was you? You'd be a prime suspect, what with your recent history with the guy. Thanks to Leslie Hanson, you probably won't even be questioned. Which is all to the good, since you won't have to answer any embarrassing questions about where you got his phone number."

"MacAullif. Just because the doorman says he talked to the congressman doesn't mean he did. What if it was the killer who answered the phone and said send him up?"

"Gee, what an excellent idea," MacAullif said, ironically. "If only the cops had thought of that. They might have asked the doorman if he recognized the congressman's voice."

"Maybe I should call 'em up and suggest it."

"Look, numbnuts. The doorman's sure. The guy was alive one minute, dead the next. Hanson's guilty, the case is over, everyone's happy. It was fun yanking your chain, but now you're becoming a drag. Get the fuck out of my office and let me get back to my other cases. Christ, I wish they were all as easy as this."

With an air of finality, MacAullif flipped the file closed on his desk.

I stumbled out of MacAullif's office in a daze.

The doorman was lying. MacAullif was absolutely right about him knowing the congressman's voice, and not mistaking it with the killer's. But he hadn't done that. He'd made the whole thing up out of whole cloth. Because it was the supercilious son of a bitch's *job* to announce all visitors. But he didn't always do it. If he'd seen the guy before, and knew where he was going, he didn't always bother. But he'd never admit that. Because it was his job to do it. And he could lose his job for *not* doing it. And he wasn't going to say he *hadn't* done it. So, he lied and said he'd rung upstairs, when in point of fact he hadn't. Because if the congressman was dead, the congressman couldn't answer the phone and say it was okay for Leslie Hanson to come up. And under the rules of the building, the rules the doorman was supposed to follow, Leslie Hanson would not have been allowed to go up.

So the doorman had lied to protect his wrinkly old ass, and the fact it put someone on the hook for a murder they didn't commit was just too damn bad.

I could burst his bubble. I could get the son of a bitch fired.

Of course, what I could get myself would be probably somewhat worse than that.

It was the worst of all possible worlds.

28

RICHARD WAS, AS I'D EXPECTED, AS SARCASTIC AS MACAULLIF. Only better informed.

"So. You hold a human being's fate in your hands. That's tricky."

"What would you do, Richard?"

"I'd get a retainer before I did anything. This looks like it could get messy."

"I mean if you were in my position."

"I wouldn't be in your position. You got yourself in the soup by working on a case after you'd been effectively fired."

"I wasn't fired."

"I said *effectively* fired. After the per diem ran out. You were working on a case for nothing for the benefit of no one. Basically, a high-risk, low-reward situation. Not surprisingly, you find yourself in a moral and ethical dilemma, teetering on the brink of disaster, with no hope of financial gain." Richard shuddered. "It creeps me out just to think about it."

"Fine, Richard. What should I do?"

"Check with Janet. She's got some cases you could work on."

"I don't mean for you. I mean for me."

"That's a rather selfish attitude. After all, I'm the one paying you."

"I get the point. I need the money. I'll do the work. Now. The dead congressman case. Legally, how am I obligated?"

"Are you kidding? You left the scene of a crime. Legally, you have to go to the cops and turn yourself in."

"Yeah, yeah. We've been over that. Legally, how am I obligated to this poor schmuck who's taking the rap?"

"If he were my client, you'd be obligated to come forward. Since he isn't, there's some wiggle room."

"For what?"

"I don't know. It's just nice that there is. The doorman is definitely perjuring himself, is that right?"

"It would appear so."

"I don't see that there's any question. You can't talk to a dead man, can you?"

"There's a small possibility he was actually on the phone with the killer, and didn't recognize it wasn't the congressman's voice. But I don't think it's likely."

"Neither do I. So, the doorman's vulnerable. Any attorney worth his salt ought to be able to rip him apart on cross-examination."

"Could you?"

"I thought that was implied."

"Suppose this guy's attorney's any good?"

"Probably an even chance. Maybe better, if the guy's got a little money. He'll probably have a fair shot at the doorman."

"He'd do better if he knew the facts."

"Don't."

"What?"

"Don't have a creeping attack of conscience. Don't talk to this attorney. Don't give him an anonymous tip. Stay as far away from him as you can."

"I ought to talk to his client."

Richard groaned. "This is why I tell you nothing short of murder. You're the world's worst client. You practically deliver yourself to the police in handcuffs, apologizing for having inconvenienced them."

"Suppose this guy's found guilty, gets put in jail for life?"

"Considering the intelligence of the average juror, and the skill of the average ADA, I'd say that was highly unlikely."

"Suppose he got convicted of anything? How could I live with myself?"

"I don't know how you live with yourself now."

"I'd have to do something."

"You haven't thought this through, have you? There's ten times more evidence against you than there is against this contractor schmuck."

Richard shook his head. "You'll wind up on a murder charge even *I* can't get you off."

29

ALICE WAS MORE SYMPATHETIC. DEVASTATINGLY SO.

"I know just how you feel," she said.

"You do?"

"Of course, I do. You feel like you should save this guy at all costs."

"You don't think I should?"

"Not at all costs."

"Where do you draw the line?"

"Don't be dumb. The point is, you're not talking absolutes. You want to save him, yes, but at what cost to yourself?"

"That's stupid."

"Oh?"

"You can't look at it that way. It's absolutely heartless."

"Suppose you could save him by sacrificing me. Would you do it?"

"That's absurd."

"Not at all. You were talking absolutes. If you're taking absolutes, I get to concoct any contradictory premise. It's only fair."

"Fair to whom? Let's get back to reality. Whether I save Leslie Hanson will have no effect on you whatsoever."

"I won't care if you go to jail? You make me sound absolutely heartless."

"This isn't *about* you."

"I see that. Clearly you're not thinking of me at all."

"Do you *want* me to send a man to jail?"

"Oh, I'm sure you won't do that."

"Then I have to come forward." I acknowledged her ironically. "Which you have pointed out would be a totally selfish act."

"Oh, well, twist my words if it makes you feel any better. Go ahead and sacrifice yourself for this lout. He is a lout, isn't he? At least he's not a model citizen. He was bribing the congressman for political favors."

"So he should go to jail for murder?"

"No, *you* should. Because the guy came to bribe a congressman and was unlucky enough to be a victim of circumstance, you should sacrifice yourself to save him."

"The guy wasn't unlucky. I called the cops on him."

"You call that lucky? And you didn't call the cops on him. You just called them."

"It doesn't matter how you spin this, Alice. The point is, I put the guy's neck in the noose, and I have the power to save him."

"My hero! May I touch you?"

"Wish you would."

"Hey! What happened to saving the planet?"

"It can wait."

"Stanley! Pay attention! Concentrate! We've got to get you out of this predicament."

"Now I'm in a predicament?"

"Didn't you say you were?"

"Yes, but you wouldn't acknowledge it. According to you, I should let the guy fry."

"Bad paraphrase. If you're going to misquote me, at least keep the gist of what I said."

"Okay. *You* tell *me* what you meant."

"I meant what I said. If you alibi this guy, you're slitting your throat. Only a moron would do it."

"So I should let him fry. Which you just bawled me out for saying a minute ago. And here you are advocating it."

"I'm *not* advocating it. I said you were twisting my words. You were twisting them then, and you're twisting them now. I don't see how we can have a decent conversation if you keep telling me what I said when it isn't what I said."

"Fine," I said in exasperation. "Would you please explain to me how *don't save him* is not the same as *let him fry?*"

"I didn't say that, either. Good Lord, you're bad at this. I didn't say don't *save* him. I said don't *alibi* him. Don't go to the police. Don't go to his lawyer. Don't go to him. Any of those moves is suicide. Don't throw yourself under a bus to save him. That's all I was saying."

"How can I save him if I don't?"

Alice smiled, spread her arms. "Finally! Through the Socratic method, a breakthrough. A moment of clarity. A revelation. I can't believe how long it took me to get you to ask that question."

"What are you talking about?"

"Oh. Never mind. Cancel that revelation. Tell me, are you losing brain cells, or were you this stupid when I married you?"

"Each body I find lowers my IQ geometrically. Give me another chance. *How can I save the guy without throwing myself under a bus* was right. Now, I'm stupid for not saying, Oh! That's the answer. I have to figure out a way to save him *without* giving him an alibi."

I smiled at Alice. "How's that?"

Alice gave me her best deadpan. "I'll call Mensa."

30

HE WAS ON DUTY. I COULD SEE HIM FROM DOWN THE BLOCK, resplendent in his uniform. He looked, if anything, slightly better groomed, just in case some TV reporter might want an interview. I wondered if he'd actually filmed any. I hadn't watched the local news at eleven. Alice and I prefer to get our news from Jon Stewart.

Anyway, there he was, the eyewitness who cooked Leslie Hanson's goose. The eyewitness who could cook mine. The man I couldn't see.

I walked up to him and said, "Hi."

He recognized me, even without the flowers.

"Hey, it's the stud. Back again."

I smiled. "You know how it is."

I'm not sure he did. But he wanted to *appear* like he did. The man actually winked.

"Is Mrs. Finnegan in?" I asked him.

"Yes, she is. You want me to ring her?"

"No, I don't."

He frowned. "Huh?"

I leaned in confidentially. "It would be awkward. She doesn't know my name."

"Oh. I see." The conspiratorial smile got wickeder. "I could say the flower delivery man."

"I don't have any flowers."

"But you're the flower delivery man."

"I don't think that's how she'll remember me."

"But she must know you bought flowers."

"It would be awkward."

"You don't want to go up?"

"Yes, I do."

"Then I have to ring and tell her."

"Trust me, she won't complain."

"So you say. You're not the one taking the risk. If I get in trouble, it's no skin off your nose."

I put up my hands. "Okay. When you're right, you're right. I see what you're saying. You're taking a risk for no reward." I took out a twenty-dollar bill. "Have a drink on me, I swear it will be all right."

He eyed the money covetously, but he made no move to take it, and an edge crept into his voice. "You don't understand. There was a murder. A couple of days ago. I think it was the day you were here. You probably heard about it. Congressman got killed in his apartment."

"Oh, yeah. They got the guy who did it, right? That was here?"

"Sure was. I spent the whole day talking to the cops and the landlord and the union rep. Not the time to be breaking rules."

"I guess not." My eyes widened. "Did you see the guy who did it?"

"Sure, I did. That's why I had to talk to the cops. I had to pick him out of a lineup and everything."

"A lineup?"

"Yeah."

"Was that hard?"

"Piece of cake. I got a good memory for faces. Just like I remembered you. I saw him go in. I knew who he was."

"He'd been there before?"

"Sure."

"Wow," I said. "This is like a *Law & Order* episode."

"Yeah," he said. "I was thinking that."

"Were you here when the cops came?"

"Sure was. Cops came, said someone called in a disturbance. First thing I heard about it. They didn't have the name, but they had the apartment number."

"They call up and ask?"

"They told me not to. Said they'd go up and see. First thing I know, more cops come, and an ambulance, and the medics, just like on TV."

"They arrested the guy right in the apartment."

"Yeah. Dumb schmuck didn't have the sense to leave."

"You were there when they brought him out?"

"Sure. Marched him out in handcuffs. Right through the lobby. The body, too. Brought it out on a gurney. Couldn't see it, it was under a sheet. They wheeled it right through the lobby into the ambulance."

"And then the cops questioned you?"

"Not right away. They had to do all that crime scene stuff. When they got around to me, boy, they were thorough. Dragged me down to the station. Union had to call someone in to take my shift."

"You get paid for your time?"

"Damn right, I did. One thing the union's good for. Something like that, beyond your control, you don't lose out. You get paid, the relief does, too."

"What about the landlord?"

"What about him? I bet he files an insurance claim, gets it all back. Insurance company's the only one takes a hit."

"Uh-huh. So, you can't let anyone go upstairs without ringing anymore."

He frowned. "What do you mean, *anymore*? I *never* do that."

"Oh. I thought—"

"You thought what?"

"Well, you said you couldn't do it for me because of this thing that happened. This guy getting killed. So, I thought if he *hadn't* gotten killed, it might be cool."

"Well, you can see it *isn't* cool. So, there's nothing I can do. If you wanna go up, I gotta ring. You wanna go up?"

I shook my head. "I imagine Mrs. Finnegan's had enough excitement for one week."

31

THE OTHER THING I COULDN'T DO WAS TALK WITH LESLIE
Hanson's lawyer. I figured that meant in person. Luckily, Alexander
Graham Bell came up with a wonderful invention.

"Hello?"

"Hello. Is this Mr. Englehart?"

"Yes. Who is this?"

"Are you the attorney for Leslie Hanson?"

"Yes, I am. With whom am I speaking?"

"I may have some information that will be of use to your
client."

"Really? Why don't you come in and tell me about it?"

"I'd rather talk on the phone."

"All right. With whom am I speaking?"

"You're speaking with someone who has information that may
help your client."

"Anonymous tips are worthless."

"Really? The way I hear it, that's how your client got busted."

"Who told you that?"

"You know your problem as a lawyer? You're too concerned with *who*, and not enough concerned with *what*. The origin of the information isn't *nearly* as important as the information itself."

"You're clearly not a lawyer."

"Is it that evident? Usually, I have to miscite a few precedents."

"If this is a crank call, I don't find it funny. My client's being held on a murder charge."

"He couldn't make bail? What happened? Is all his money tied up in your retainer?"

"I'm going to hang up now."

"The doorman's lying."

"What?"

"The doorman. In the apartment building. At the crime scene. The one who ID'd your client. He's lying."

"You're clearly not familiar with the facts of the case. My client was arrested at the scene."

"Yeah. Always a bad move. I'm surprised you didn't advise him against it."

"The doorman's identification of my client is irrelevant since my client was found there."

"That's not what he lied about. He lied about calling upstairs and the congressman saying to send him up."

"And you know that how?"

"From the facts. You'd know it, too, if you weren't so damn arrogant. Does your client say the doorman called upstairs? Does your client say the doorman talked to the congressman?"

"What my client said is none of your business."

"No, but it should be yours. Your client is a frequent visitor in the building. Ask him if the doorman *made him wait* while he called upstairs, or if he just sent him up and called to say he was coming. If it was the latter, ask him how he knows the doorman called at all. He doesn't, and the doorman didn't. He only says he did so he won't get in trouble with the landlord and the union. But he didn't bother calling up, and if he had, the congressman wouldn't have answered because the congressman was dead. If he says the congressman was alive when your client went up, he's lying."

"How do you know that?"

"Because I can reason," I said. "See, I never went to law school."

32

THIS TIME MACAULLIF WAS *REALLY* PISSED.

"To what do I owe your indignation?"

"What do you think?"

"I don't know, MacAullif. Are you playacting this time? Because, I must say, once was funny, but if you're going to make this a regular thing . . ."

MacAullif slammed his fist down on his desk. "Don't fuck around. What did I tell you about the congressman?"

"He may have been accepting bribes."

"Don't play dumb. It's typecasting, and you're still no good at it."

"Hey. I used to be an actor. That's just cruel."

"You wanna see cruel? Stick around. I'll show you cruel."

"To what do I owe this ill humor?"

"The Congressman Blake case."

"Oh, good. I have nothing to do with that case. Who are you mad at?"

"I just got a call from the ADA assigned to the case. He's fit to be tied."

"Oh?"

"The congressman's attorney slapped a subpoena on one of his witnesses. Wants to take his deposition."

"Can he do that?"

"No, he can't do that. He can't interrogate a prosecution witness under oath before the trial. The attorney knows that."

"So, it's a stupid move."

"No, it's a brilliant move. It's a red flag that the witness is lying. It makes the prosecutor say, 'What the fuck am I getting myself into.' Then he takes a good hard look at his witness and tries to figure out what the lie might be."

"What'd he come up with?"

"I didn't bring you in here to give you information. I brought you in here to bawl you out."

"I kind of got that impression."

"Do you know *why* I'm bawling you out?"

"Not enough bran in your diet?"

"Out of the clear blue sky this dipshit attorney decides to take a pass at a prosecution witness."

"I don't want to tell you your business, MacAullif, but some lawyers would consider the phrase *dipshit attorney* actionable."

"I have to wonder where the attorney got the idea."

"Gee. You don't suppose *his client* confided in him, do you?"

"His client didn't know anything. His client was a dumb schmuck got caught in the act. He's gonna tell his attorney, 'Hey, the doorman who let me up is probably lying, because I wasn't there at all.'"

"That doesn't seem likely," I admitted.

"So, I'm just wondering if you happened to talk to Leslie Hanson's attorney."

"I haven't been anywhere *near* Leslie Hanson's attorney."

"Did you talk to him on the phone?"

"I'm going to have to refuse to answer on the advice of a dip-shit attorney."

"Yeah," MacAullif said with disgust. "The last time I had you in here, I didn't think you knew enough to make trouble in this case. Turns out you do. Which is bad news on all counts. Forget the fact you're a meddling pain in the ass. If you knew enough to tip off Hanson's mouthpiece, then you are mixed up in this *way* more than you let on. Perhaps even made that phone call to the police."

"Oh, for God's sake. You're still afraid I'll get you in trouble over the phone number."

"I'm *not* afraid you'll get me in trouble over the phone number. I'm afraid you'll get convicted of murder trying to get the contractor off the hook."

"I think you're overreacting."

"*I'm* overreacting? Fine. Then tell me. Yes or no. Did you make that phone call to the police?"

"Do you really want to know?"

"Of course, I do."

"If I'd made that phone call to the police, I would have had perfectly pure motives. And no idea anyone might be at the scene of the crime."

"Really? The phone call reported an altercation. Can you have an altercation without at least two people?"

"Well, now you're taking the phone call at face value, MacAullif. Don't a large percentage of these things turn out to be cranks?"

"It wasn't a crank. The guy was dead."

"That does add validity to the complaint. Even so. If some moron found the congressman dead, and didn't want to report it themselves because it would get them in trouble, they might make a bogus nine-one-one call, reporting an altercation in progress, which was, in fact, already resolved. Would that be illegal? I mean, *failing* to report a crime's illegal. But *inaccurately* reporting one? That can't be so bad."

"Is that what you're saying you did?"

"Don't be as dumb as I am, MacAullif. That's what I am very carefully *not* saying I did."

"Jesus Christ!" MacAullif's face ran the gamut from insane fury to utter hopelessness, with a number of stops along the way. By the end, the poor son of a bitch resembled one of those droopy dogs that have far too much skin and look like they need their face ironed out. "If you found the body, the whole house of cards comes tumbling down. You had to get in there, which means the doorman probably saw you. Is that right?"

"We're talking hypothetically here."

"I don't care *how* we're talking. This is one fucking mess."

"That was sort of my assessment of the situation."

"So, it turns out you did every fucking thing I brought you in here to bawl you out for."

"Allegedly."

"Allegedly, hypothetically, I-don't-give-a-flying-fuckedly."

"I don't think that's a real adverb."

A vein I never realized MacAullif had bulged out of his forehead. "Not good at reading social cues, are you? This is no fucking joke, asshole. If what I think happened happened, then you are teetering right on the brink of a one-way ticket up the river."

"You're mixing metaphors." I put up my hand. "Sorry. Reflex action. Point taken. I'm totally fucked and there's no way out. Now, you wanna help me or blame me?"

"I'd like to kick your fucking ass from here to Hoboken."

"I can see that. Right now I'm a little busy, but maybe later we could arrange it. Meantime, how can I get out of this mess?"

"Easy. Go home. Lock your door. Disconnect your phone. At least let the answering machine pick up. Stay as far the fuck away from everyone as humanly possibly. For God's sake, don't try to fix anything. You can't do it. All you can do is drag yourself down, and everyone around you."

"Come on, MacAullif. I can get that type of advice from my wife. I thought I was talking to a cop."

His mouth fell open. "You arrogant schmuck. If ever there was anyone with less reason to be cocky, I haven't met him. Despite it all, you still think you can fix this thing."

"I don't think I can fix this thing, MacAullif. I think, like you say, it's all gonna come down on my head. When it does, I'd like to see you don't get hurt. Apparently, you don't care about that."

MacAullif shook his head. "It's like talking to the wall. You got a situation, the minute you stick your neck out, you're fucked. The minute I stick *my* neck out, *I'm* fucked. I can show a passing interest in a case that has nothing to do with me, but that's it. Anything more, people want to know why."

"You met the congressman at a fund-raising dinner."

"The congressman's dead."

"And you're pissed, after paying for dinner."

MacAullif exhaled. "Jesus Christ."

"Lighten up. I don't expect you to do anything. You dragged me in here, remember. To bawl me out. Which you've done admirably. I stand rebuked. I'll take it from here."

"No. You *won't* take it from here. You won't take *anything* from *anywhere*. You will stay way the fuck away from this case, do you hear me? You'll leave the cops alone, and you won't go near them, will you?"

"Absolutely not, MacAullif. And this ADA who complained to you . . ."

"Yeah?"

"What's his name?"

33

ADA REYNOLDS WAS ONE OF THOSE HOTSHOT ATTORNEYS too young to live. MacAullif hadn't given me his name, by the way. Instead, he had set what had to be new decibel records for One Police Plaza. I'd looked the guy up on my own.

Reynolds squinted at me. "What's your name again?"

"Stanley Hastings."

"And what's your interest in the case?"

"If you check police records you'll find I got caught up in a little caper involving the congressman. He brought his son's teenage girlfriend down to Philly to see the kid perform in a boy band. I was duped into thinking he'd picked up a teenage prostitute. It was a setup. I was supposed to blow the whistle on him and make an ugly scene. Instead, I got the girl away from him and brought her back to her parents. Naturally, all parties were pissed as hell, and I come out looking like a schnook. That's fine, getting suckered is part of the game. But when I see on TV the guy got

148

killed, I can't help thinking it's gotta be connected. The guy got scammed. It didn't work, so he got killed. See what I mean?"

The young ADA had a look on his face like I was trying to sell him the Brooklyn Bridge. "And you got no reason for thinking this."

"I just told you one."

"That's not a reason. That's a wild guess."

"It's an educated guess."

"Oh, please."

"Look. It's none of my business. I did my job, I got paid. But I can't help thinking there's a connection. I give it to you for what it's worth."

"You're aware I've made an arrest?"

"So I hear. You confident of a conviction?"

"That's a strange way to put it."

"Sorry. I was trying to look at it from your point of view. You think you got the right guy?"

ADA Reynolds frowned. "You think I don't?"

"I have no idea. That's why I'm asking you. This other thing happened I thought you should be aware of."

"Is this a matter of record?"

"I don't know. The congressman may have hushed it up. Assuming such things can be done."

"Uh-huh," the ADA said, ironically. "And just what would the congressman have hushed up, now?"

I gave him an abbreviated version of my adventure. I left out such things as chloral hydrate, and both my abortive and my successful attempts to get into the congressman's building. Even so, it was quite a story.

ADA Reynolds was not impressed. "You were hired by the mother of a teenage hooker. Only she wasn't the mother and the girl wasn't a hooker."

"I admit it sounds bad."

"Bad? Do you have any idea what a defense attorney could do with this? This could add two weeks to the trial, and give some numbnuts juror a reason to vote not guilty."

"May I quote you on that?"

"Look. Thank you for coming in. You've done your civic duty. Now, you want to do me a favor, go drop off the face of the earth. I can't afford these extraneous matters entering the case."

"You're sure they're extraneous?"

"We know what time the congressman got home, and we know what time his body was found. In between those times, one, and only one, person went up to his apartment. He was arrested in the apartment with the dead congressman. Now you can't ask for a simpler case than that. All this other stuff is just a distraction."

"You know what time the congressman got home?"

"Yes."

"How?"

"I don't have to present my case to you."

"No. You can send me away and let me give my story to the newspapers."

His face darkened. "Son of a bitch."

I put up my hand. "I don't wanna do that. I just want to assure myself I'm doing the right thing. Believe me, if this guy is guilty, I'd be very happy. I just want to be sure. So, how do you know when the congressman got home?"

ADA Reynolds was torn between stamping his foot at the nasty man spoiling his fun and having me arrested for being an asshole. "We have surveillance video of the apartment building garage. It is timed and dated. The congressman's car drove in a ten forty-five. The congressman's body was found at two fifteen. Between ten forty-five and two fifteen the only person who went up to see the congressman was the suspect in custody. You wanna argue with that?"

"Ten forty-five and two fifteen?"

"That's right."

"Doorman never went to lunch?"

He frowned. "What makes you ask that?"

I shrugged. "Trying to think like a defense attorney."

"During the doorman's lunch break the porter's on the desk. The porter didn't see anyone go up, either."

"Good, reliable witness, the porter?"

"I believe him."

"What's his name?"

"None of your business."

"How about the doorman. Good solid witness?"

"Absolutely."

"Interesting."

"What?"

"With the porter, you just believe him. With the doorman, it's *absolutely*. I was wondering why the emphasis."

"The doorman's a much more important witness. Seeing as how he sent the guy up."

"Uh-huh. And he's sure of his story?"

"Of course he is."

"Can I talk to him?"

"No, you *cannot* talk to him. You're not to go anywhere *near* him, you understand? If I find out you've been messing around with my witness, there'll be hell to pay. Are we clear?"

I put up my hands. "Hey, hey. No need to get nasty. You made your point."

34

ALICE WAS IMPRESSED. "YOU FINESSED THE ADA INTO keeping you away from the doorman?"

"That's right."

"By pretending you wanted to see him?"

"I wasn't pretending. I do want to see him."

"Yes, but not under your right name in front of the ADA. That would complicate things."

"No kidding."

"So, you pulled off a bit of reverse psychology, and you feel pretty pleased with yourself."

"It worked."

"Yes, it did."

"Yes. And even if it is only a variation on Br'er Rabbit's 'Don't throw me in the briar patch,' it's still impressive."

"It's been a long time since Br'er Rabbit."

"Yes, it has. I suppose I should give you credit." Alice frowned.

"I'm just not exactly sure what for. Let me see if I've got this straight. You're celebrating the fact the ADA in charge of the case is not going to confront you with the doorman because of your clever scheme, which involved going to the ADA and pretending you wanted to contact the doorman. What I'm not getting is the ADA would never have thought to confront you with the doorman, in fact would never have known you were involved in the case at all, if you hadn't gone to him in the first place."

"I was afraid you'd see that flaw."

"Stanley, this is not a game. Someone is dead. Someone else in charged with the crime. It has nothing to do with you. Yet you seem to delight in tiptoeing on the brink of discovery. What was the point of going to his ADA?"

"I've opened lines of communication."

"For what? To get yourself arrested? To get yourself indicted? How far are you going to take this? You can't show up in court. The doorman will recognize you. He may not be the brightest guy on earth, but he's gotta wonder what the flower delivery guy's doing there."

"It's not going to get to court."

"Why not? What you gonna do, confess?"

"Alice. I don't think you're giving me enough credit."

"I'm sorry. You're a hero. You're very brave, standing up to that big ADA."

"I'm not just making sure he doesn't confront me with the doorman. There's the whole bit about me tailing the congressman. If the ADA sniffed it out, he'd haul me in, put me on the carpet. If I go in, throw it in his face, say, 'Hey, look at this, I got a right to be here,' his gut reaction is, 'No, you don't. None of this stuff has anything to do with the case. Get the hell out of here.' Now, maybe that's just the briar patch again, but damned if it didn't work."

Alice yawned and stretched. She looked gorgeous. "Work how?

I'm getting a little confused. Was your entire purpose prophylactic, or are you trying to solve this crime?"

"You shouldn't say prophylactic to a horny PI."

"Stop that. Aside from getting the guy who hadn't noticed you to not notice you, what did you accomplish in terms of the case?"

"I met the guy. Now, if I come up with something, I got a place to take it."

"Oh, my God," Alice said. "You're not Br'er Rabbit. You're Raskolnikov, helping the cop in *Crime and Punishment*."

"I'm not like Raskolnikov."

"Why not?"

"I'm not Russian."

"Stanley."

"And I didn't kill the pawnbroker woman. Come on, Alice. Someone killed the congressman and someone set me up. If it was the same person, don't you think I'm a danger to them? Don't you think I should be on my guard?"

"Absolutely. You should do absolutely everything in your power to assure them you are not a danger to them and they should not rub you out. Now, where does going to the authorities fall in that category?"

"Well, if you're going to nitpick."

"Come on. Get serious. Going to the ADA is a stopgap measure at best. It doesn't advance you any in terms of the investigation"

"So?"

"You say you're just laying the groundwork. Fine. You laid the groundwork. Lines of communication are open. You're prepared to set your plan in motion. So, what's your plan?"

"Plan?"

35

I DIDN'T HAVE A PLAN, AT LEAST NOT ONE THAT I COULD tell Alice. Because whatever I came up with, Alice could poke holes in it. Alice is good at that. I wouldn't stand a prayer.

The congressman had a wife and kid. I'd seen the kid. I hadn't seen the wife. If she turned out to be the woman who hired me, everything would fall into place. But I didn't see how that could be. Not if her intention from the beginning was to knock hubby off. She would have to appear at the funeral. She would have to suspect I would, too. At least if I were in any trouble over the little caper. And how could I not be? By rights I'd be arrested in Philly. Which tends to tick people off. I could be expected to show interest in the parties involved. Meeting the congressman's wife would be highly likely. Not to mention finding her picture in the paper, or seeing her on TV. Neither of which I happened to do. Still she couldn't be sure of that.

I wondered if I should interview her. On what pretext, I had no idea. Of course, if she was the woman who hired me, it wouldn't matter. I'd ID her, and that would be that. But if, as it felt likely, she wasn't, I would be up shit creek without a plausible reason for asking.

It occurred to me it was probably better just seeing the woman without talking to her. But where? She'd have to go to the funeral. But she'd be the grieving widow. You'd have to pay your respects to the grieving widow. It was only polite.

However, Congressman Jason Blake was a pubic figure. His memorial service was announced in the paper. Lots of people would go. It would be easy to get lost in the crowd. No one would notice me.

I put on my best suit, took Alice for protective coloration. And she's observant where I'm not. Alice didn't know any of the parties involved, but I could count on her insights. All right. More observant *and* smarter. Besides, she wanted to go. Probably just to keep me out of trouble.

I had no trouble spotting Valerie Blake. The congressman's widow was dressed in black and accepting condolences.

"Is that her?" Alice said.

"Yeah, that's the congressman's wife."

"I know *that*. Is it the woman who hired you?"

"Not in a million years."

"You sure? You're really bad at faces. And she's dressed in mourning."

"It's not her."

"The kid with her is the one you saw dancing?"

"I assume so."

"You assume so?"

"I couldn't ID him if my life depended on it. A boy band, for Christ's sake. They're plastic, like Ken dolls."

While we watched, a girl came up to him, squeezed his hand.

"That's the daughter," I said.

"Really? She doesn't look like a hooker."

"Alice."

"That's the girl you rescued from a fate worse than death?"

"Hey, give me a break. If you thought someone was abusing her, would you do something about it?"

"I think I'd check it out first."

"How?"

"I don't know. But I would. Before I drugged and abducted her."

It was a no-win situation. I kept my mouth shut.

The girl left her boyfriend, returned to an older couple in the front row.

"That's her parents?" Alice said.

"Yes. Jennifer and David Weldon."

"Who *do* know you, and would freak out if they saw you here?"

"That's right."

"So, we probably won't be talking to them. You recognize anyone else here?"

I didn't. Of course, I was hard-pressed to, being apolitical, at least on the local level. I voted early and often for Obama.

The only other one I recognized was Sharon's cheerleading friend, whose name I couldn't recall, standing with her parents, whom I'd never met, a skinny, mousy woman and a rather athletic-looking man. I figured it was Daddy, frustrated without a son to play quarterback, who pushed his daughter into cheering the team.

Aside from them, I was lost. I spotted a couple of girls I might have seen in the movie theater, but if I had to swear to it, I couldn't.

Granted, I didn't know the congressman well, but as far as I was concerned, his memorial service was a washout.

Then I spotted him.

My heart leapt. My mouth fell open.

Alice said, "Great poker face. Who is it?"

"That's him."

"Who?"

"That's the guy. Son of a bitch! I did it."

"*You* did it?"

"That's the defendant. His lawyer got him out of jail."

"Damn!"

"What do you mean, damn?"

"Are you a moron? We talked about it. If he's off the hook, they'll come after you."

"They won't come after me. Because of the briar patch."

"That only worked while they had a suspect," Alice said, impatiently. "Now they'll come after everybody."

"They won't come after me."

"Damn it, what the hell is he doing here?"

"Paying his respects."

"Oh, sure."

"Well, he knew the guy."

"He was accused of *killing* the guy," Alice said.

"Yeah, but he didn't do it. He probably liked him."

"Even so, he shouldn't be here. Will he recognize you?"

"As the flower delivery guy he saw coming out as he came in? I doubt it."

"Didn't you deliver the flowers?"

"Yeah."

"So you didn't have them when you came out. So he wouldn't peg you as a flower delivery guy. Just a guy leaving the building."

"I suppose."

"So, if he did recognize you and saw you here, he might say, 'Hey, this guy was coming out when I came in. And he's at the congressman's funeral. So he was probably calling on him.'"

"He won't recognize me."

"I hope not. If he ID'd you there'd be hell to pay. Particularly after your briar patch story. The ADA would put two and two together and—"

"All right, all right. I'll keep a low profile."

"I would keep it right down on the floor."

Luckily Alice and I were in the middle of the crowd, and Leslie Hanson was pushing his way toward the front.

"You don't suppose he's going to pay his respects to the widow?" Alice said.

He was. Leslie Hanson got in line behind the people waiting to see the congressman's wife.

He was next in line when she saw him.

Her eyes widened. Her face paled. I could see her lips mouthing the word, "You!"

Leslie Hanson put up his hands, took a step toward her.

Bad move.

The congressional widow let out a savage scream of anger and dread.

The room fell silent. Everyone froze, transfixed by the horrific tableau of the congressman's killer crashing his memorial service to threaten his wife.

Who would save her?

Sharon's father lunged to his feet, but her mother pulled him down.

There was no need.

The contractor had taken a step back. The widow's shrieks had crescendoed and died. The crisis was averted.

Nearly.

The athletic-looking father of Sharon's cheerleading pal, though somewhat slow on the uptake, was, once roused, not at all reluctant to act. He lunged across the room, hurtled into the air in a headlong dive, and pinned the startled contractor to the floor.

36

RICHARD WASN'T PLEASED TO HEAR FROM ME. "WHO'S DEAD?"

"Congressman Blake."

"Again?"

"Still."

"And why, in the name of God, would that warrant my attention?"

I gave Richard a rundown of the memorial service. He wasn't impressed. "You weren't arrested?"

"No."

"This numbnuts defendant was?"

"That's right."

"Last time I checked, he wasn't my client. Isn't it a fact the damn fool was stupid enough to hire some vastly inferior defense attorney to represent him?"

"I think that's true."

"You're qualifying your answer? Is that because you're not sure he hired some other attorney, or you think the guy might possibly be good."

"Richard—"

"I thought I made myself clear. When they arrest *you* for a homicide. Not every moron who comes down the pike. He's got an attorney. I can't act in his behalf. It wouldn't be ethical. I don't care what the situation is. I can't do a damn thing for him."

"I don't expect you to do anything, Richard. I just needed a legal opinion. If you want to suggest someone who'd know better . . ."

"Oh, very clever. Play to my vanity. Is that what you're doing?"

"No, Richard. I just need some advice."

"Why? You weren't arrested. You're free and clear."

"True, but if I'm not careful I might be, and then I'd have to bother you, and it'd be more than just a phone call. It would be coming down to the police station and getting me out of the hoosegow, and maybe going to trial."

I shouldn't have said that. Richard likes to go to trial. But it was all right. A hypothetical courtroom battle couldn't outweigh hours of drudgery, sifting through layers of legal bullshit. "What's your damn question?"

"What can the police arrest him on?"

"They arrested him at the service?"

"They hauled him out in handcuffs. Basically just for being there."

"Was there a restraining order?"

"I bet there will be now."

"But there wasn't then?"

"Not that I know of."

"How can I answer the question if I don't know the facts?"

"All right, there wasn't."

"How do you know?"

"Because no one would have thought of it."

"That's not legally binding."

"No, but you can take it to the bank. Hell, I bet no one expected the guy to make bail."

"That's thin, Stanley."

"Why are you arguing a technicality?"

"That's what lawyers do."

"Fine. Take the hypothesis there was no restraining order in place. The guy was out on bail. What law was he breaking by going to the memorial service?"

"That would depend."

"On what?"

"On what he did there."

"He didn't do a damn thing. He got in line to see the widow. The minute he got close enough for her to recognize him, she started screaming."

"Did he make a move toward her?"

"He took a step back. At which point he was wrestled to the ground by a good samaritan."

"Define good samaritan."

"Jock-type friend of the family with more brawn than brains. Cops came, arrested the defendant for provoking an altercation."

"Oh. So you *do* know what he was arrested for."

"No, I don't. That was a surmise on my part. Just a generalization."

"Do you expect me to offer legal advice based on surmises and generalizations?"

"Come on, Richard, I need some help. I can't talk to MacAullif."

"And your wife's too smart for you."

"Exactly."

"I was kidding."

"Then you don't know my wife. Come on, help me out."

"With what? Much as I hate to admit it, you seem to have a fairly good grasp of the situation. From what you tell me, the guy was within his legal rights, was arrested on no provocation whatsoever, and may have a case of false arrest. I would be stunned if his attorney doesn't file one. But it's got nothing to do with me. And it's got nothing to do with you. I'm still not sure what you're asking."

"Okay, say this guy was your client."

"Yeah?"

"How would you go about getting him off?"

"And there it is! Backed into a corner, you finally ask the question you've been avoiding the whole time. You want a defense strategy."

"It's not that I *want* one."

"No, of course not. You just want to know that one exists. So you won't feel like you dorked the poor son of a bitch."

"It's worse than that, Richard."

"Really? How can it be worse than that?"

"I want to do something."

"Of course you want to do something. It's the least logical course of action for anyone with any sense of self-preservation. Naturally, that's where you'd want to go."

"All right. Let's suppose I was *not* a totally self-destructive flaming asshole. What can I do that doesn't utterly jeopardize my life, liberty, and pursuit of new clients for the law firm of Rosenberg and Stone?"

"Well put. You been saving that up? Because you rattled it off like you had it memorized."

"That doesn't make it any less true. Look, I got a situation here where I can't approach the parties in the case without fear of exposure of having been at the scene of the crime. The only one I met in person is the ADA in charge, and I did such a good job of convincing him to give me a wide berth that I can't really go back. So, say you were defense attorney in this case. Aside from slapping a subpoena on me, what would you do?"

"I would get a cash retainer."

"Richard."

"Guys like this, you do a lot of work and the check bounces."

"Anytime you're through having fun."

"All right. Never mind what an attorney would do. Let's talk about what you could do."

"What do you mean?"

"It's a ticklish situation. Why don't you go over your relationship with the principals in this case, and let me know which ones of them you can actually approach."

"So you can advise me?"

"No, I just think it will be amusing." When I said nothing, he added, "Yes, of course, so I can advise you. The fact it's amusing is just an added perk. Okay, let me have a whack at it. You can't see the defendant because he might recognize you as the guy he saw leaving the building. That goes double for the doorman, who thinks you're an amorous flower delivery boy. Plus another doorman who wouldn't let you look at the surveillance video when the congressman drove the girl into the garage."

"Actually, that would be okay, since I told the ADA about it."

"That was the ADA who you *can* see, unless he gets the bright idea of putting you in a lineup for some of his witnesses."

"Why would he do that?"

"I have no idea. But if you keep nosing around in this case the way you're threatening to, it would seem entirely likely. Then you got the girl herself. Whom you accosted on the street and later drugged and abducted. That would seem like a no to me. How does it seem to you?"

"You're not helping, Richard."

"The girl's parents are probably also nonstarters. How about the jock who tackled the guy at the memorial service? You ever meet him?"

"No, I didn't."

"How about his wife?"

"Her either."

"They've never seen you in the course of this case?"

"Not as far as I know."

"So, you'd be safe contacting them."

"Ahh . . ."

"Ahh?" Richard groaned. "What have you done this time?"

"I haven't done anything. It's just you say would I be safe contacting them. Probably. I never met either one of them. Only thing is, their daughter's friends with the other girl. I've seen the two of them together. I don't think she saw me."

"Why not?"

"I was conducting clandestine surveillance."

"Oh, God! We can assume she has your name, address, phone number, and your picture on Facebook. Fine. For safety's sake, say you can contact them without the girl. That would seem a logical course of action."

"Why?"

"Why? Good Lord. You want advice, or you want me to think for you? Macho Man tackled the defendant. Either he's a dumb jock who just likes violence, or he had a reason. What reason might a brawny young man have for impressing a recently widowed woman?"

"You think he was hitting on the congressman's wife?"

"Wanted to hit. Was hitting. Had hit. Say he was her lover and he knocked hubby off. Isn't that a typical film noir plot? Say he did, and then the dingbat construction worker stumbles on the body and gets arrested for the crime, and lover boy's delighted to see a scapegoat take the rap. Only at the service, rude surprise, here's the guy, free as air, showing up to protest his innocence. Macho Man snaps, and attacks him in a furious rage."

"You think that happened?"

"How the fuck should I know? Jesus, you want a lot for your money. Considering you're not paying any. You wanted someone you could approach and something you could investigate. There you are."

"I suppose."

"You don't sound happy."

"Hell, Richard. The guy's rather peripheral."

"Peripheral? Good Lord. Only a total asshole would ask for free advice and then complain that it's peripheral. Okay, you want something a little less peripheral? Would that satisfy you?"

"Like what?"

Richard cocked his head.

"Ever meet the widow?"

37

I'M NOT BIG ON WIDOWS. I DON'T KNOW THE RIGHT THING to say. I don't know the right thing to do. I know I shouldn't look at their breasts, but beyond that . . .

I'm not talking memorial service, of course. I know the protocol there. You take their hand, mumble something unintelligible, and move on.

But afterward, once a young woman is launched out into the world with a big W on her forehead, what then? Do you compliment her clothes, her hair? I suppose it depends on what she's wearing. If she isn't wearing all black, is she fair game? I don't mean to make advances, I mean to talk to like a normal person.

Approaching attractive women of Alice's age—and here we must tread lightly, for anything I say I am in deep shit. In fact, I am in deep shit for merely mentioning Alice. But I am talking about a woman old enough to have a teenage son. A hot mom, if you will. And, therefore, a hot widow. Gee, good thing I reminded myself not to look at her breasts, I could have gotten lost in a whirlwind of sexist thought.

Aside from the protocol, there was the plausible lie. What the hell reason did I have for talking to this woman? I mulled it over and the best I could come up with was none. I had no reason whatsoever for bothering the woman. It occurred to me I needed Dortmunder and the rest of Donald Westlake's comic crooks to plot the thing for me.

I called Alice, asked her to Google Valerie Blake, widow of Congressman Blake. I didn't mention any idle speculation over the widow's age.

Alice looked it up while I held the phone. Valerie was a graphic designer for Farrel and Lynch, 675 Madison Avenue.

I had hung up before it occurred to me to ask Alice what Farrel and Lynch was. I considered calling back. The amount of abuse Alice would subject me to for forgetting to ask wasn't worth it.

I drove over to Madison Avenue, lucked into a parking meter, and went in. The office building had a doorman at a desk. In some of them you had to sign in, but not here.

"Farrel and Lynch," I said.

He jerked his thumb. "Seventh floor."

"What kind of firm are they?"

He looked surprised. "Good firm."

Well, it was worth a shot. I got in the elevator, rode up to seven. The sign on the glass door read: FARREL AND LYNCH, GRAPHIC DESIGN. So, Valerie was not a graphic designer at an ad agency. She worked for an agency that specialized in graphic design.

The reception area was large for the number of people in it. There was a couch, a few chairs, none occupied. It had a stainless steel, glass, and leather look, or whatever synthetic material was fashionable for the leather look these days. It occurred to me I was rather ill prepared for this interview.

Behind a circular plexiglass desk, a woman with too much makeup was chewing gum and reading a fashion magazine.

Granted, I'm a novice, but I'd have designed her differently. On the other hand, she was perfect for my purpose. I walked up, stood in front of the desk.

She finished the paragraph she was reading, looked up, and said, "Yes?"

I flashed her a smile. "Valerie Blake?"

Her face fell. Not a good poker player. "Is she expecting you?"

"I believe so."

"What's your name?"

"Steve Harrison." I read in some detective story when giving a phony name to use your initials so no one will notice you have a different monogram. The fact I have nothing monogrammed hasn't persuaded me to break the habit.

The receptionist consulted a ledger on her desk. "I can't find your appointment. Did you confirm it with her?"

"No. Actually, her husband is the one who set it up. He said she'd call if there was any problem, otherwise just come by."

"Her husband."

"Yes. I'm sure he told her about it. I guess she didn't tell you."

The receptionist made a face, shook her head. "I don't think he did."

"He wouldn't forget. He's very good at those things."

"Mr. Harrison. Congressman Blake is dead."

"What!"

"He was killed. A couple of days ago. In his apartment. Surely you must have seen. It was on all the news."

"I've been out of town. Killed. Do you mean . . . by someone? You mean he was murdered?"

"Yes."

"Do the police know who did it?"

"Some contractor. Someone he had dealings with."

"When did this happen?"

"Tuesday."

"Tuesday?"

"Tuesday afternoon. The police arrested the killer in his apartment."

"Oh, my God. I just spoke to him that morning. About the appointment. No wonder he didn't tell her. Except he was going to call her on the phone."

"I don't think so."

"Why not?"

"She was out that morning. Most of the time. Didn't get back until after lunch."

"Are you sure?"

"The police asked. I don't know why. They had the suspect in custody. Valerie was back shortly after lunch. Had an appointment with a client. Right here in the book. I wrote it down, and I checked it off. She had appointments all afternoon. Right up until the police called."

"That satisfied the police?"

"Oh, yeah."

"So her one o'clock appointment wasn't with anyone suspicious."

"Suspicious? Huh-uh. Advertising firm. Long-standing client. So, you want me to ring her?" the receptionist said. Her manner clearly implied she hoped I didn't.

There I was at the crossroads, needing a quick decision. A poor position for one who wrestles with things in his mind. What could I learn from seeing Valerie I hadn't learned from the receptionist? All I was apt to do was blow my cover. Which seemed entirely likely, considering my knowledge of advertising graphics and my fictional relationship with her husband.

I had just talked myself into skipping the meeting when the widow herself walked out. She'd shed her morning garb, and looked good in a tan business suit. Not a pantsuit, but a tan jacket and skirt, the latter just a tad on the short side, not indiscreetly so, but enough to warrant attention.

"Oh, Ms. Blake," the receptionist blurted. "This gentleman's here to see you."

She frowned. "Really? Who are you?"

I couldn't remember my name. At least I couldn't remember the one I'd given the receptionist. Talk about blowing your cover! That had to win a prize. Who the fuck was I?

Just in the nick of time, I remembered the monogram.

"Steve Harrison. I'm so sorry about your husband. I had no idea. If I'd known, I certainly wouldn't have come."

"Thank you." She frowned, realizing nothing I'd said had answered the question. "And why are you here?"

"I'm so sorry. This is a horrible misunderstanding. Jason was going to tell you. Of course, he didn't. He suggested I see you."

"Yes, I see." She clearly didn't. She looked around helplessly, as if slightly overwhelmed and not sure what to do with me. "Would you mind stepping into my office for a moment. I don't have time for this meeting, but let's straighten things out."

"I could come back later."

"No, no. I need to tie up loose ends. Please. Just for a minute."

"All right."

I followed her down the hall into a small but well-lit office where a drafting table was titled up to show the layout for what appeared to be a whiskey ad. Logos and text were missing.

She saw me looking, said with exasperation, "Yes. It's due tomorrow. I'm way behind. I know they'll make allowances, but I don't *want* people making allowances, you know what I mean?"

"Yes."

"So, what do you want?"

I gestured to the drawing board. "This. I need a layout for an ad."

She nodded. "What venue?"

Gulp. Venue? The first thing that came to mind was, "Venue wish upon a star," which couldn't be right.

I covered by clearing my throat. "Magazines."

That seemed to satisfy her. "What's the product?"

"Perfume."

"Perfume?"

"For men."

She frowned. "Perfume for men?"

"For gay men."

I wondered if that would red-flag it as bogus. Apparently not. She just nodded and said, "Stated or implied?"

"Huh?"

"Anything in the ad say gay?"

"We don't use the word."

"Of course not. I mean pronouns, like *he* or *him*. 'Will he like you in it?' 'Wear it for him.' If it's a man's perfume, the pronoun says gay. Hell, I don't have to tell you this, right?"

"Right."

"So what's the slogan?"

"Slogan?"

"Oh, come on. You want me to write the ad or design it?"

I put up my hand. "Sorry. I'm shaken by the circumstances. The slogan is, 'You look good, why not smell good?'"

She winced. "I don't know. That's so bad it might be good. You know, like Oder Eaters. How soon you need this?"

"There's no rush. It isn't on the market yet." I took a breath. I'd gotten this far, and I was on shaky ground bluffing ad copy. Might as well dive in. "Look, I can't believe Jason is dead. What happened?"

"Didn't Jeanie tell you?"

"Jeanie?"

"The receptionist."

"She said someone killed him. I can't believe it."

"I know. But he was a politician. They make enemies."

"What do the police say?"

"They caught the guy who did it."

"So the investigation's over."

"His lawyer made a fuss and they let him go."

"They let him go? Then they must have doubt."

"I don't think so."

"Well, did they hassle you?"

"What do you mean?"

"I'm sorry. I shouldn't have said anything."

She looked at me sharply. "Don't do that. I can't stand that. Start to say something, and then decide you better not. What did you mean?"

"Nothing. It's just when the police have to let a suspect go, they start looking for someone else."

"How do you know that?"

"Books and TV. I just wondered if they bothered you. It would be cruel, but that's how they are. Did they ask where you were at the time of the murder?"

"No. Of course not. Why would they do that?"

"No reason," I said.

But there was. And they *had* asked, according to the receptionist. And the widow had denied it. Rather vehemently, in my opinion.

I backed my way out of the office, promising to leave my name with the receptionist, and thanked my lucky stars I'd managed to get through the meeting. Gay perfume as a cover story? What would an analyst do with that? Maybe I should market it. 'You look good, why not smell good?' Just because I didn't have a product didn't mean I couldn't whip up a little interest. Hell, I could probably make a bunch of internet sales before anyone noticed.

I gave the receptionist a phone number that would have been unlikely to reach Steve Harrison even had he existed, and got the hell out of there, having successfully pulled off a broad-daylight, pre-frontal assault on the congressman's widow. She hadn't told me anything, but from the firm's receptionist I'd gleaned what I needed to know. Valerie Blake had gone out for a meeting, stayed out until after lunch. Perfectly innocent on the one hand, and yet it afforded her all the time needed to conspire with a killer to do hubby in.

Only trouble was, she hadn't gone into the building. At least, according to the doorman and the porter on the desk during lunch. Still, there was wiggle room. A person plotting a death would take pains not to be seen. I just had to figure out how it could be done.

I rode down in the elevator feeling pleased with myself. I nodded at the doorman at the desk who'd assured me Farrel and Lynch was a good firm.

I went out the door and nearly stopped dead.

Granted, lobby meetings mean nothing. Hey, it's an office building. People pass in the lobby, no big deal. Still, I was super-sensitive having passed Leslie Hanson in the lobby of the congressman's apartment building, just before the dumb schmuck got nabbed for a killing I knew he didn't do. A killing I knew for certain happened earlier than his arrival, perhaps even as early as before Mrs. Congressman got back from lunch.

So, while the presence of two people in the lobby of an office building by no means implied they were going to see the same person, or even the same office, or even the same floor, still it was enough to register a huge blip on my oh-my-God-what-the-fuck's-going-on meter.

The man coming into the office building where the congressman's widow worked was Macho Man, the superjock, who only yesterday, at Congressman Blake's memorial service, had executed a beautiful flying tackle to bring the congressman's alleged killer down.

174

38

RICHARD RAISED AN EYEBROW WHEN I POKED MY HEAD IN the door. "Yes."

"I got some more information."

"About the congressman killing?"

"That's right."

"Have the police charged you with it?"

"You know they haven't."

"I don't know any such thing. You're perfectly capable of talking yourself into a murder rap."

"Well, I didn't."

"Then why are you here?"

"Come on, Richard. Aren't you interested? You're the one who said to talk to her in the first place."

"You talked to the congressman's wife?"

"Yes."

"On what pretext?"

"I was afraid you'd ask me that."

"Your fears are justified. What did you tell her?"

I gave Richard a rundown of my gay perfume campaign. I can't say he seemed interested in investing.

"You fed her that line of crap and she didn't see through you in an instant?"

"It's a hard time for her. Her husband just got killed."

"And what did you learn from this clever subterfuge?"

"The day hubby was killed the widow was out of the office until after lunch. The police asked her about it. She denies it."

"She denies she was out until after lunch?"

"No. She denies the police asked her about it. Now, why would she tell me that?"

"More to the point, why would she tell you anything? Here's a moderately intelligent young businesswoman spilling her guts to the first moron through the door."

"Yeah, but she had a reason."

"What?"

"She was rattled, and she wanted to get me out of there."

"Why?"

"Aha!" I said.

I told him about Macho Man.

He wasn't impressed. "The father of her son's classmate came into her office building? What a revelation! Better start fitting him for the handcuffs."

"This is the man who attacked the man who killed her husband. More to the point, this is the man who attacked the man *accused* of killing her husband, who probably didn't do it. Which opens up a whole bunch of possibilities."

"Are any of them going to make me money? Stanley, I got cases to file, summonses to serve. Or, rather, to have you serve. I don't have time for your theories."

"But you sent me to her."

"To get you out of my office. Not to have you come right back."

"I just thought you'd be interested."

"You thought wrong. This is all very nice, but none of it adds up to squat. You have the thinnest plot threads imaginable. You are weaving them together with wishes." Richard paused. "Hmm. I may try that on a jury. Anyway, I can't see how anything you accomplished merits a trip to my office. From where I sit, it adds up to one thing. You've made no progress, and you're hoping for help. Well, guess what? I'm fresh out. I gave you the widow. If that's a good lead, something will come of it. If it's a bad lead, you'll work that out. But some leads don't pan out, and some cases don't get solved. That's life. But it's not your fault, and it's certainly not mine."

The phone rang. Richard snatched it up, said, "Uh-huh . . . Uh-huh . . . Okay, okay, give me a minute, I'll be right out." He hung up. "Sorry to cut this short, but I have a client."

"That's okay. I think I got the gist."

I started for the door.

"Stanley."

"Yes?"

"If you wouldn't mind, go out the side door. I don't want you bumping into my client in case you meet up in court. Could be awkward at the voir dire. 'Have you and the other parties ever met?' You know how it is."

"Yeah, right. You're just embarrassed by me."

As I went out the side door it occurred to me to wonder why *would* he care if I met a client? Was he embarrassed by me? What was that all about? As Alice and/or a good therapist would point out, when things aren't going well paranoia sets in.

On the other hand, paranoid people have enemies.

I was in the back hallway by the service elevator. I slipped down the corridor, pushed open the door to the front hall. At the far end was the glass door reading ROSENBERG AND STONE. Through it I could see the switchboard, manned by Janet of Wendy/Janet fame.

I tiptoed down the hall, peered through the door. The waiting room was empty. Either Richard was lying about his client, or he'd shown him in the minute I was gone. I considered asking Wendy. But that was a double-edged sword. She'd rat me out to Richard on the one hand, give me bad information on the other. If I wanted to know, I'd have to wait.

I waited, and I don't know why. There was just something in his voice. The way he handled the phone call. He hadn't said "Tell him to wait." He hadn't said, "Ask him to sit down." In fact, he hadn't referred to a client at all. Only to me, and only after he'd hung up the phone. So what kind of a fast one was he trying to pull? Assuming he was trying to pull anything at all. And I wasn't just weaving wishes, or whatever the hell it was he expected to dazzle juries with.

I only had to wait ten minutes, and there was Richard, appearing at the front door, pulling it open, holding it for the client. Which made it one hell of a client. Richard doesn't hold doors for anyone. He points his finger as people open doors for him. So, who was this client too important for me to meet, and important enough for Richard to hold the door?

The client stepped out, and I ducked back behind the bend of the hallway.

The client wasn't a client. No surprise there. Richard's clients barely rated the time of day, and when they got it, it came from Wendy/Janet. Few clients ever met Richard. Those who did met him in court, where the sum total of his advice was to keep quiet and let him do the talking. So his claim that a client had come to his office was a dead giveaway. I quite expected him to walk out with Mayor Bloomberg, or such like.

Wrong again.

Richard's client, with whom he apparently had a dinner date, was none other than Ms. Fairfield, the attractive young ADA who'd busted me for the congressman caper.

39

ALICE WAS IMPRESSED. "RICHARD'S DATING AN ADA?"

"Yes."

"He seduced her to get you off the hook?"

"Somehow I doubt it."

"Yeah, but it's a nice thought. It's above and beyond the call of duty. And you didn't even give him a retainer."

"Alice."

"He's not charging you, is he? I mean, if those should turn out to be billable hours . . ."

"I'm glad you think it's funny."

"Of course it's funny. And original. You've never had your lawyer date your prosecuting attorney before."

"She's not my prosecuting attorney."

"Thanks to Richard. I do like him so much better for this. Makes him almost human. Instead of some sort of robot into which you put a quarter and a lawsuit comes out. Say, that could be a new children's toy. A cause-of-action figure."

Alice was on a roll, which was good. When Alice was on a roll, things were either good, or very, very bad. There was no way the situation with the congressman slipped into the very, very bad category. No one suspected me of having anything to do with the congressman's death. And there was little likelihood anyone ever would. Even the doorman, my worst-case scenario, couldn't put me in the apartment. There probably weren't enough inferences to hold me for questioning, unless I voluntarily spilled my guts. If arrested, I would just say, "Call my lawyer. If you can't reach him, page your ADA."

"So," Alice said, "Richard was no help."

"No."

"He figured he'd given you all the help he could, now it was up to you."

"That's not exactly how he put it."

"He pooh-poohed your theory about the widow and the jock."

"Pretty much."

"Do you think he's right?"

"I don't know."

"So, what's your plan?"

"What do you mean?"

"Who you gonna go to next? Besides me. See, I can't help you much."

"You're always a help."

"You just say that because you want sex."

"What's your point?"

"What are you going to do?"

"I don't know."

"That's the problem. You want someone to tell you."

"I'd settle for the sex."

"Why can't you see MacAullif again? Not the phone number, that's ancient history. I mean the most recent reason."

"I tipped Hanson's lawyer off the doorman was a bad witness."

"Oh, right. Which pissed off the ADA, and MacAullif figures it was you. That's so unfair."

"It happens to be true."

"Yeah, but he doesn't know that."

"I sort of implied it."

"No wonder he's pissed."

"A moment ago it was so unfair."

"A moment ago you hadn't implied it."

"So I can't talk to MacAullif. So what do you think I should do?"

"Talk to MacAullif."

40

"DON'T THROW THAT!"

MacAullif had picked up his phone. I don't mean the receiver, I mean the whole damn thing. He was holding it as if it were a baseball and I were a batter he was about to brush back from the plate.

"I'm not here on police business. Or private eye business. Of any other business. I got some juicy gossip."

MacAullif is not an old woman. He is a hard-nosed homicide cop. He put down the phone. "What gossip?"

I told him about Richard and the ADA.

MacAullif frowned. "What's the ADA's name?"

"Fairfield."

He frowned. "Fairfield?"

"She's a woman and she's pretty."

"That's sexist. You think there aren't a lot of pretty ADAs?"

"Of course not. That would be sexist."

"You want me to throw this phone at you?"

"I'd rather you didn't."

"What's she look like? Never mind. I remember the composite you did with that sketch artist."

"She wasn't Asian," I volunteered.

"Well, that narrows it down. Was she black?"

"I don't think so."

"You're a trained investigator. You'd have probably noticed."

It was a relief to see MacAullif horsing around, even if it was on a safe subject, far removed from the case in question. I wondered if I should bring it up?

"How long you gonna dick around before you ask me about the case?" MacAullif said.

I grimaced. "I don't know what to ask."

He exhaled. "Oh, for Christ's sake. Just like old times. Here you are, totally clueless, looking for a lead."

"Actually . . ."

"Yes?"

"I got some more gossip."

"Do tell."

"It has to do with the case."

"Why am I not surprised. This is the real reason for your visit, you're afraid to bring it up, so you preface it with a similar story that doesn't mean anything, and might even be fictitious. Is Richard really dating anyone, or was that just a ruse?"

"He's dating an ADA."

"Good for him. Who's the real couple you're concerned with?"

I told him about the widow and the stud.

MacAullif was actually interested. "You think the guy's ringing her bell?"

"I have no idea."

"It would open interesting possibilities."

"Yes, it would."

"Particularly if the contractor's off the hook."

"Of course, we can't assume that. Just because his lawyer got him released doesn't make him any less guilty."

"You have an annoying habit of stating the obvious."

"Sorry about that."

"I should say the obvious but untrue. Since you and I know the guy didn't do it."

"I wouldn't go that far, MacAullif. I can spin you a number of scenarios where the guy's actually guilty."

"I'm sure you can. It doesn't alter the fact he's not." MacAullif considered. "I like it. The marital triangle, I mean. It's a good motive. A lot better than some contractual dispute. Sex beats politics. Sex *and* politics beats practically anything. I don't suppose you could spin that, could you? This jock isn't a political figure?"

"I don't know anything about him."

MacAullif grimaced. "And this is the extent of your investigation."

"I'm a little hampered here, MacAullif. The number of people I can approach in this is rapidly dwindling."

"Not fast enough," MacAullif grumbled.

"You'd rather I didn't bring you this?"

"I'd rather you brought me some facts. Rather than a recitation of who you happened to meet in what lobby. Couldn't you have found out anything?"

"If I had, you'd be all over me for poking around in a case where I've got no business."

MacAullif looked like he might pick up the phone again.

"You see my problem. The widow thinks I'm one person. The widow's son's girlfriend thinks I'm another. The widow's son's girlfriend's parents—"

"Oh, stop it," MacAullif said. "I get the point."

"Do you? The doorman thinks I'm someone else. The ADA thinks I'm me but doesn't know who I am. I mean in terms of my actual involvement and motivations."

"I could tell him. You're a major pain in the ass." MacAullif exhaled, shook his head. "Listening to you whine, I would say there were two ways you could go. You could slip the ADA a tip to lean on this jock. In terms of effectiveness, that would rank about zero. Or you could try to make it make sense. You got a whole bunch of disjointed facts. What you gotta do is find a point where it all hangs together. Right now you got nothing. See what I mean?"

"Uh-huh," I said. "So you're telling me you've got no advice?"

I was out the door before MacAullif hefted the phone.

41

I THOUGHT OVER WHAT MACAULLIF HAD SAID, ABOUT
finding a place where it all came together. That wasn't much help.
The unifying factor seemed to be the murder of the congressman.
That brought everyone together, but only to the extent they were
involved. It seemed to me I had the ingredients in place; I just had
to stir the pot. The question was how. As I told MacAullif, I had so
many personas kicking around in this little caper it was difficult for
me to come and go. I was reminded of the Kurt Vonnegut short
story about the very shy actor who merged into the parts he played
but had no real personality of his own. That was me all right, the
shy, ineffectual detective, wondering *Who Am I This Time?* And what
could I do. Of all MacAullif's suggestions, such as they were, the one
I liked best was the anonymous tip. Of course, that would be my
favorite, involving no real action on my part. Just give the ADA the
idea and let nature take its course. Only how much credence was
the guy going to put in an anonymous tip? They must get a hun-

dred a day, any one as credible as mine. Would he act on it? Not likely. And, if so, was there any way to investigate the possibility without being so blatantly obvious that everyone knew exactly what he was going for, and had no problem evading the issue.

No, an anonymous tip was out.

Luckily, ADA Reynolds and I had a relationship. It wasn't all that bad. The guy knew me as me. Maybe he didn't know who the me he knew was, and maybe my intentions were couched in duplicity. But he didn't know that. As far as he knew, Stanley Hastings, private eye, was an unlucky son of a bitch eager to wash his hands of the whole affair.

I went down to the courthouse and hunted up the ADA. That's not as easy as it sounds. The guy didn't just have that one case, he had a lot of cases, spread out all over the court system. Today he was presenting a case to a grand jury. Not the congressman's case, but another case, about mishandling securities, which was probably very important to those people whose securities were mishandled but which somehow seemed tame next to a murder. I waited for him to break for lunch, which he had to do by one o'clock, since the grand juries change, the morning shift moving out, and the afternoon shift moving in. That's the good thing about grand jury duty. It's only half a day. The bad thing is it lasts a month.

I met him in the hall, walked him back to his office. He didn't seem pleased to see me. At least he didn't call the cops. "Can you make this fast? I got a luncheon date."

I told him about Macho Man. I can't say he thought it was earth-shattering news.

"The guy from the memorial service showed up at the widow's office. And this concerns me how?"

"Suppose he didn't just happen to protect her. Suppose they were having an affair."

"Shocking. Who gives a damn? Except some tabloid reporter. Do you know for sure that they were?"

"No."

"Do you have *anything* else to indicate this guy might be involved?"

"Not in itself."

"Not in itself. God, I hate that expression. Do you have anything that is *not* in itself?"

"Well, if the evidence should indicate the contractor didn't do it . . ."

"Do you have any evidence that would indicate the contractor didn't do it?"

"Not in itself."

"Here we go again! What evidence of *any kind* do you have that the contractor didn't do it?"

"Well, you let him go."

"Not because he's innocent. Because his lawyer made a fuss. Jesus Christ, lawyers try everything they can, not because their client's innocent, but because they're getting paid."

"I understand. Still, if the case was airtight, I don't think he'd walk."

"He didn't walk. He's out on bail."

"Pot*ay*to, pot*ah*to," I said.

He glared at me. "How do you happen to know this guy showed up at her office?"

"Oh."

"Oh? What's the deal?"

"I thought I should pay my respects."

"You saw the widow at her office?"

"That's right."

"And she didn't throw you out?"

"Oh."

"Oh?" He said. His voice rose ominously at the end of it. "She didn't know you were the private eye trying to catch her husband with teenage hookers? So who *did* she think you were?"

"Oh."

"It gets worse and worse, doesn't it? You called on the widow in her office and pretended to be who?"

I gave him my gay perfume cover story.

He listened incredulously. "What the hell are you doing? You don't have a client. No one's paying you. You have no interest in the case? Why are you involved?"

I had no answer, so any interruption was welcome.

Almost any.

"What's *he* doing here?"

I turned and looked.

My mouth fell open.

ADA Fairfield stood in the doorway, makeup on, purse in hand, every bit as alluring as she had been the night before when she'd been going out with Richard.

My mind had a lot to process. This woman knew me from the congressman caper. She also knew Richard was my attorney. But she didn't know I knew she'd been out with Richard. And she didn't know, until this moment, I had anything to do with ADA Reynolds. Now she did, and in the general scheme of things, that was not good.

Luckily, her question was not addressed to me. I kept quiet, let ADA Reynolds handle it.

"Oh, right," he said. "You caught the congressman thing, and this is the guy."

"Yeah. What's he doing here?"

"He has theories."

"Oh, he does, does he? And what might they be?"

"He thinks the contractor's innocent."

She turned her eyes on me. I felt the way a mouse must just before being devoured by a snake.

"He thinks the congressman's wife is having an affair with the father of one of her son's playmates, and that the two of them conspired to do hubby in."

"Has he been drinking?"

"Not that I know of."

She digested that bit of information. "How does he gather this information?"

"You wouldn't believe."

The attractive ADA didn't believe. As ADA Reynolds explained the situation, she looked at me as if I were from another planet. "You know much more than you should."

"I wish you'd tell my wife. She thinks I'm clueless."

"You're clearly not clueless. You're just not very bright. Constantly throwing yourself at the ADAs in charge." She considered. "Is there anything you might be afraid of?"

"I'm afraid the cops might screw around and never solve the case."

She grimaced. "See, that's the problem. The only way that makes sense is if you knew the contractor wasn't guilty."

"Oh, bullshit," I said. "Sorry, but I'm tired of being used as a punching bag. The cops made a knee-jerk reaction, arrested the guy at the scene of the crime. No one has taken the time to see if he might have been there legitimately."

"Kind of hard to have a legitimate meeting with a dead man," she said. "You're awfully concerned with this. How come?"

"You know how come. I got duped into setting the congressman up. From where I sit, it looks like when they couldn't frame him, they killed him."

"What makes you think the two things are related?"

I shrugged. "It seems like a lot of bad luck for one guy."

She gave me a pitying look.

I put up my hand. "Okay, forget it. I just thought I should pass along the information. In the future, I'll keep my ideas to myself."

I turned and walked out the door. Wondered if they'd let me. Not that they could stop me. They weren't cops, they were lawyers. But they could at least ask me to come back.

They didn't. I made it down the hallway, turned the corner, exhaled, and leaned against the wall to let my heart stop racing. Talk about bad ideas! Dealing with one ADA was risky enough. Dealing with two was suicidal. I was lucky to walk out a free man. How long I remained that way was another matter. I wondered if they'd have me stopped in the lobby. Paranoid thinking, yes, but I had a lot to be paranoid about.

The problem was, the ADAs' assessments were right on the money. If my story was true, if I wasn't holding out on them, if I was telling what I knew, then there was absolutely no reason for me to be there. Which there wasn't. Aside from knowing the man they were prosecuting wasn't guilty. And the most likely way to know he's not guilty would be if I was. All and all, it was a miracle they let me go.

I had just had that thought when they came around the corner.

I nearly jumped a mile. Damn, here I was marveling at my escape, and they got me anyhow.

Only they didn't. They swept right on by and rang for the elevator. She looked up at him with sparkling eyes. Then I noticed his arm was around her waist.

Son of a bitch.

She was his date.

42

I HAD RUN INTO AMOROUS ADAs TOO CAUGHT UP IN THE throes of their own passion to realize I was delivering myself to them on a plate. And one of them had been out with my attorney the night before. What was the etiquette? What was the protocol? I'd been a married man so long I don't even know.

I was reminded of the old Everly Brothers song "Should We Tell Him?" To let him go on trusting wasn't fair, but, on the other hand, it was none of my business. Unless the bitch was playing him for a reason. Which made no sense, because the reason would be me, and I'd just presented myself to her, signed, sealed, delivered, and she hadn't seemed to give a damn. Perhaps she was just a working girl who liked to eat. I wondered what young ADAs made these days. Probably more than I did. Of course, they'd have years of student loans to pay off. Maybe she just liked dinner. Maybe she just liked Richard. Whatever the reason, I was getting nowhere fast, and no one seemed to want to help me.

So what should I do now? Piss in a bottle, call it gay perfume, and go bluff the congressman's wife? That seemed like a high-risk, low-yield plan.

I called Hanson's lawyer. "I see you took my advice."

"Huh?"

"Your client's out walking around. I guess that tip on the doorman paid off."

"My client's out walking around because he's innocent."

"Save it for the press. You know and I know your client's out walking around because you made a stink about the doorman's story and the ADA backed down. So don't give me that my-client's-innocent shit. I'm more responsible for getting him out than you are."

"Now, look here—"

"Want some help? You still need it. There's a big difference between being out on jail and being found not guilty."

"I'll get him off."

"Oh. Bad quote. Sounds like a shyster. What you meant to say is, 'My client is innocent and a jury will surely agree.'"

The lawyer's voice was cold. "What do you want?"

"I want to help you. If you don't want my help, that's fine. But it's free. At that price, it's hard to beat."

I could hear him take a breath. Then he said calmly, in measured tones, "And how can you help?"

"Got another tip. Take it or leave it. What you do with it is your business."

"What's the tip?"

"The congressman's wife may have been a little too friendly with one of the family friends."

"Who?"

"Guy who tackled your client at the memorial service."

"Him? He's just a dumb jock."

"Yeah," I said. "And women never fall for those."

43

I WAITED FOR TWENTY-FOUR HOURS FOR THE LAWYER TO stir the pot. It didn't get stirred. No arrests, no threats, no splashes in the news. I was beginning to lose faith in my powers as an investigator. I'd done a few cases for Richard, each one drearier than the last. I threw myself into them eagerly, hoping the money I earned would go toward the rent and not the potential and ever increasingly more likely necessary Stanley Hastings defense fund.

Finally, I could stand it no longer. I called Hanson's attorney. "What happened with the jock?"

"Nothing happened with the jock. I called, said I wanted to take his deposition. He said sure, he's coming in tomorrow."

"What about your client?"

"He's innocent."

"Aside from that."

"Haven't heard from him."

"Since when?"

"Yesterday. Why?"

"You tell him about the anonymous tip?"

"That's funny."

"What's funny?"

"Calling it an anonymous tip. You made it. It's not anonymous to you."

Leave it to a lawyer to split hairs. "Fine. The tip. You tell him about the tip?"

"What do you think? I'm taking a deposition and billing him for the time. I'm not going to let him know?"

"That was yesterday?"

"Yes."

"You haven't heard from him since?"

"No."

"You try to call him?"

"I called him, he wasn't in."

"You leave a message?"

"Yeah, but he didn't call back. It wasn't urgent."

I hung up on the attorney, gave the client a call. Got the answering machine. I didn't leave a message.

I hung up and called Alice. "Wanna look up Leslie Hanson's address?"

"Why?"

"He's not answering his phone."

"Maybe he's not home."

"It's a cell phone."

"So what?"

"Guy's lawyer can't reach him. You don't hide from your lawyer."

"You do if you owe him money."

"You trying to kid me out of it?"

"Well, let's see. The guy's been charged with a murder you know he didn't commit. Telling him would make you the prime suspect instead. Yeah, I'm trying to kid you out of it."

"It isn't working. What's the address?"

Leslie Hanson lived on Third Avenue in a fourth-floor walk-up over a pizza parlor. I rang the bell, got no answer. Considered ringing other apartments, see if anyone buzzed me in. Considered loiding the lock with a credit card, had visions of it snapping off with the part that said Stanley Hastings imbedded in the door. Considered taking a step back and kicking the damn thing down.

While I was thinking all that, a young man on his way out actually held the door open for me.

I went in, took the stairs up to Hanson's apartment. On the last flight I realized the phrase *fourth-floor walk-up* should have been a deal breaker.

As I reached the top, it occurred to me I now had to get into the apartment. I was running through my list of choices again when I noticed something funny about the door. The shadow being cast on the frame seemed to indicate it was ajar.

I walked down the hallway, pushed on the door.

It swung open.

I stuck my head in, called, "Leslie."

I don't know what I expected. Him tied up in bed perhaps, unable to reach the phone. If so, he was also gagged, because there was no answer.

The apartment was dark. I groped for a switch, found one on the wall just inside the door. Flicked it on. I was in a small, haphazardly furnished living room. Leslie might be a contractor, but he wasn't an interior designer. His furniture might have been gathered off the street. None of it matched in period, style, or color. I have no taste in apartment furnishings, as Alice often reminds me, but even I could tell everything clashed. It made me hesitate a moment. Was it really worth sticking one's neck out to save a man with so little taste?

The bedroom had all the charm of the living room, enhanced

by an unmade bed. Dirty socks and jockey shorts adorned the floor.

On the far wall, the door to the bathroom beckoned. I wondered what atrocities it held.

Just one.

The body of Leslie Hanson hung from the shower rod.

44

HE WAS FULLY CLOTHED IN A GRAY SUIT, WHITE SHIRT, THIN tie, black leather shoes. The rope around his neck was ordinary clothesline. It was a wonder that it held. Evidently he had tied it around one of the faucets in the tub, run the rope up over the shower rod, then stood on the edge of the tub, pulled the rope as tight as he could, and then tied it around his neck. It was tied in a single knot, which on first glance appeared to be a square knot but on closer inspection proved to be a weak granny knot, a square knot's poor relation, looped the wrong way. Hanson had apparently tied the knot and stepped off the side of the tub. The tension in the rope was just sufficient to keep his toes from touching the floor. A gagging man touching solid ground would have instinctively stopped himself from choking, no matter what his intentions. But his feet hadn't reached the floor, which would have left him, had he had second thoughts, with only the hope of grabbing the rope to pull himself up to take the tension off his neck, a ploy which, had he attempted it, clearly hadn't worked.

On the bathroom mat, directly below the body, was a sheet of paper.

I leaned in to take a look.

Written on the paper were two words: I'm sorry.

My sentiments exactly.

It was, in my opinion, the clumsiest attempt to make a murder look like a suicide imaginable.

I took a quick look around the bathroom, didn't see anything else significant. I went out though the living room, trying to remember what I'd touched. As far as I could tell, it was only the doorknob. I hated to wipe it off. I might be eliminating the murderer's fingerprints. On the other hand, if the murderer was stupid enough to leave fingerprints, they'd probably catch him anyway. I took out a Kleenex, wiped the doorknob. Wondered if they could get DNA from mucous. Snot possible, I told myself. That was enough to tell me I was losing it again.

I slipped out, left the door in the position I'd found it, and got the hell out of there.

I hurried down the street, trying to remember what the guy who'd let me in looked like. Another in a growing list of people I had to avoid. I found a pay phone, dropped in a quarter, and called nine-one-one.

The operator who answered sounded bored. Even the report of a dead man didn't perk her up.

I hung up the phone, got in the car, and drove home.

On the way, I promised myself for the umpteenth time never to second-guess Alice again.

45

I FELT TERRIBLE. I'D TRIED TO HELP AND ONLY MADE THINGS worse. What an understatement. I'd gotten a guy killed, that's what I'd done. By sticking my nose in where it didn't belong, I'd basically murdered the contractor. The guy hadn't hung himself. Not unless he was a suicidal acrobat. No one teeters on the edge of the tub trying to knot a noose, no matter how attractive the alliteration. He'd been killed for following up the lead I gave him through his attorney.

Which more or less solved the case. The jock killed the contractor. Which meant the jock killed the congressman, bang, over, finished. I was right, but it was small consolation. I was also a killer.

Alice knew something was wrong the minute I came in the door. "You look terrible. What is it?"

I told her what happened.

She was predictably sympathetic. "It's not your fault."

"Yeah, it is."

"No, it isn't. You had vital information in a murder case. It was your civic duty to pass it along. It would have been obstruction of justice if you hadn't."

"How can you say that? You told me not to."

"Because you didn't know if you were right. Turns out you were. So your information was important."

"You can't spin this, Alice. I fucked up and a guy is dead."

"I know. And all the poor schmuck wanted to do was bribe a congressman."

"You saw him. At the memorial service. You think he deserved to die?"

"That's not the point. Things happen for different reasons. They're all intermeshed. Did what you said to his lawyer have anything to do with him getting killed? Maybe. But would he have gotten killed if he hadn't tried to bribe the congressman? No. So don't try to take all the blame."

"I can't argue with you. You're too good with words. I grant you all the points you're trying to make. I still feel like shit."

"I know."

Alice made me some chicken soup. Funny. That's what you do for a person who's sick. In a way, I was.

She didn't talk while I ate, just saw I had napkins and a spoon. I sat at the kitchen table, ate it up.

"Want some more?"

"No."

"Feel better?"

"No."

"You have to let it alone."

"I can't."

"Yes, you can. The cops know everything you do. They don't need you. Between the ADA and the guy's lawyer, they know all they need to know."

"Not really."

"Didn't you say he filed a deposition?"

"Yes."

"Well, there you are. The lawyer was investigating the guy. The lawyer's client knew that he was investigating the guy. Who are the cops going to want to talk to? You, or the guy?"

"You should have seen him, Alice."

"No, I shouldn't. You shouldn't have, either. It's bad, but it's over. You have to leave it alone. Stay out of it, let the cops do their job."

I sighed. "Yeah."

It was on the evening news. MURDER SUSPECT HANGED. "Leslie Hanson, a suspect in the murder of Congressman Jason Blake, was found hanged in his apartment earlier this afternoon. Mr. Hanson, arrested at the scene of the crime, was currently out on bail. Hanson was discovered with a rope around his neck, hanging from a shower rod. While the police have not ruled out foul play, a note apparently in Mr. Hanson's own handwriting, found at the scene of the crime, would tend to indicate that the suspect had taken his own life in a fit of remorse."

Alice muted the TV. "Don't."

But she knew it was no use.

46

AT LEAST MACAULLIF DIDN'T THROW THE PHONE. HE snorted, said, "I was hoping it wasn't true."

"MacAullif."

He put up his hand. "Don't start with me. I'm sitting here, hoping he won't walk in the door, and sure enough, here he comes. I know what that means. It means he did something stupid I was hoping he hadn't. Fat chance, what with another anonymous tip."

"So what could I do?"

"You could stay out of my office. You could stay out of crime scenes. You could stop treating every murder as if it had been perpetrated solely to aid in your personal psychotherapy."

"I'm a bad boy. I got a lot of guilt."

"No shit. Can I assume you found this asshole's body and have been beating yourself up ever since?"

"Hypothetically?"

MacAullif waved it away. "Oh, say whatever the fuck you want.

I figure I'll lose my pension anyway, you decide to roll on me. Look, bad as you may feel, this one's over. So why don't you go home."

"That was Alice's opinion."

"Wives aren't always wrong."

"Trouble at home?"

"Yeah. My wife expects me to reach retirement, not get suspended for acting dumb. It was a nice case, but it's over."

"How can it be over? The contractor got killed."

"Oh, *that* case. I'm talking about the congressman. Hanson was going to trial for that. Now he isn't. You can't prosecute a dead man. That's how ADA Reynolds sees it."

"You're kidding."

"I'm not. I spoke to him this morning. Just to head off any trouble. Turns out there isn't any. He's winding up the case, much as he hates it. Slam-dunk conviction up in smoke. You don't get one like that every day."

"But that's not what happened."

"What do you mean?"

"Hanson didn't kill himself."

"Oh. That's another case. Still under investigation. Even if something comes of it, I doubt if Reynolds would handle it. He's fed up with the whole thing."

"Wait a minute. The cops really are writing this off as a suicide?"

"Watch your tone. Cops don't do that. We investigate based on the evidence. That's all we can do."

"What *about* the evidence? Hanson's lawyer scheduled a deposition. With this guy who was friendly with the widow. Are the cops investigating that?"

"I would imagine the deposition's off."

"No kidding. What about the jock? Are the cops talking to him?"

"Cops talked to him this morning."

"And?"

"Guy was out of town yesterday. Cleveland. Business trip. All day. Couldn't have done it."

"Any corroboration?"

"Probably airline tickets and luncheon receipts."

"No witnesses?"

"No one's going to Cleveland if they don't have to. They may have talked to witnesses on the phone."

"So the guy was in Cleveland."

"Yeah."

"But he's back in town now."

"That's right."

"But he's not being deposed."

"That would be my guess. You wanna talk to the lawyer, I can't stop you."

"Which means I was wrong."

"There's a shocker."

"If the jock's not the killer, the killer's still out there."

MacAullif grimaced, put up his hand. "Don't, don't, don't. Just because you had a bad theory proved wrong, doesn't mean you have to come up with something else convoluted. If anything, it should ease your conscience. Ratting out the jock didn't kill the contractor."

"What if it did?"

MacAullif groaned. "Well, then the laws of reason have been suspended. Look. You ratted out the jock, the congressman got killed. You think it's cause and effect. It doesn't have to be."

"You mean it's coincidence?"

"You know I hate the word. But this isn't it. It is not coincidence the guy got killed. He was involved in the murder, either as the perpetrator or the guy who got framed. In either case, there's a reason for him to die, and it doesn't have to have anything to do with you. Jesus Christ, what an egocentric asshole you are. You'd think you were the protagonist in some fucking book. Like those mysteries you read. Which is your whole problem. Real crime isn't like that, and you can't take it. But that's how it is. Someone killed the contractor. They chalk it up to suicide, they're wrong. Do yourself a favor."

"What's that?"

"Don't tell them."

47

I WASN'T GOING TO, REALLY. UNLESS IT BECAME BLATANT, flagrant, absofuckinlutely obvious, or some other superimperative that could not be ignored.

Mine came in the form of a cop inviting me downtown to talk to ADA Reynolds. I was tempted to decline, but it turned out attendance wasn't voluntary, and with Richard unwilling to intervene for anything less than a charge of murder, it seemed prudent to comply. I was also curious what the guy wanted. If he'd really washed his hands of the case, why bother?

I was in for a surprise. ADA Reynolds wasn't alone. ADA Fairfield was with him.

"Oh," I said. "You guys ganging up on me?"

ADA Reynolds said, "Don't try to be cute. This isn't funny."

"Why am I here? I thought the case was closed."

ADA Reynolds shot a look in the direction of the attractive attorney, and the situation was instantly clear. I was there because his girlfriend wanted me there.

I couldn't wait to tell Alice.

"We have some loose ends to tie up. We were hoping you could help us out."

"I don't see how. Your suspect is dead. Unless you have another suspect."

"We don't yet."

"Does that mean you're not buying into the suicide theory?"

"What suicide theory? You mean the one they're spouting on TV?"

"I thought you'd washed your hands of the case."

"Who told you that?"

Oops.

"I guess I just assumed."

"Yeah."

ADA Fairfield smiled at me. "He's just pissy because his defendant's dead. It's an unfortunate situation. We're looking into it. So far you're the only unifying factor."

"What are you talking about? I don't unify anything. I was connected to the congressman. I'm not connected to anything else."

She cocked her head. "I thought you were the one pushing the theory about the widow's lover."

"Right," I said. "And how did that pan out?"

ADA Reynolds looked at me sharply. "You sound like you know."

"Yeah, well I don't. They could be banging like bunnies or barely know each other. I have no idea which."

"It was your theory."

"Yeah. But I didn't have the resources to check it out, so I brought it to you. As you'll recall, that was before your suspect's untimely demise." I settled back in my chair. "So, tell me, does that wind up the case or not?"

"What do you think?"

"I think it's pretty damn convenient."

"Uh-huh. You know how we found the body?"

"Hanging from a shower rod."

"I mean how we *came* to find the body."

"An anonymous tip?"

"I don't recall releasing that to the media."

"Well, if it wasn't, you wouldn't be asking the question in such an insinuating manner. How *did* you find the body?"

"Anonymous tip."

"You're lucky you got it. Otherwise he might still be hanging there."

"I doubt it. His lawyer would have checked him out."

"Why? He owe him money?"

ADA Reynolds took a breath.

Once again, his girlfriend stepped in. "There's no reason to adopt an adversarial attitude. We have an unsatisfactory case. There's some things we could probably help each other with. Whaddya say?"

"I'm your man. Whaddya need?"

"For starters, what's your interest in this case? Because it's not apparently obvious. And, yet, you persist."

I sighed. "I'm a second-rate detective doing a third-rate job. I chase ambulances. For the most part. Every now and then someone else hires me. I do my best to discourage them. Sometimes the money's so good I can't resist. I did the congressman a bad turn. I'd like to think it didn't get him killed. If the contractor's the answer, I'm delighted. But I'm not going to take it on face value."

She frowned. "That's the same old song. It doesn't really fly. There's one thing that points to this not being a murder-suicide. The anonymous tip. If Hanson hung himself, who called? You say an innocent bystander who didn't want to get involved. That's all well and good. But then you go back to the killing of the congressman. And what do we find? An anonymous tip.

What are the odds of *two* innocent bystanders who don't want to get involved?"

"In this city? Pretty damn high."

"Yes, yes, that's very wry and cynical and patently untrue. The odds are pretty damn low. So low I can't see it happening."

I said nothing, sat and waited. Cursed ADA Reynolds for having a girlfriend. If the guy hadn't had a sex drive, I'd have been home free.

The predatory female stretched like a cat, prepared to pounce.

I shuddered involuntarily.

"No," she said. "It seems far more likely the same person made both phone calls."

"You mean the killer?"

"No. That makes no sense. Why would the killer care?"

"The killer wants to make it look like a murder-suicide, to make you think Hanson's the killer."

"Why? We *already* think Hanson's the killer. Nobody thinks anything else. Killing Hanson doesn't convince anyone he's the murderer. It just raises suspicions."

"Some killers aren't very bright."

"No, no. You can't have it both ways. The killer can't be smart enough to frame Hanson, and too dumb to think it through." She smiled. "But you very cleverly changed the subject. We were talking about those anonymous calls. Who could have made them *besides* the killer?"

I opened my mouth.

She continued, "Or two shy innocent bystanders. No, it would have to be someone with a vested interest in the case. Someone with the motivation to go poking around where they shouldn't. Can you think of who that might be?"

"Have you tried the widow's lover?"

She shook her head. "No, no, no. That would be a choice for the killer."

"Then I have no idea."

"That's strange. You seem to have ideas about everything else." She cocked her head. "So, you still think Hanson is innocent?"

"Yes, I do."

"How can that be? According to the doorman, he's the only one who was there."

"Aside from the obvious answer that the doorman is lying, let's assume he's telling the truth. Let's assume the congressman had a visitor who managed to get into the building despite the ironclad security of the world's best doorman. Let's assume that visitor killed the congressman. The objection is the phone call upstairs. If you reject the obvious answer that the doorman is lying, let's assume he called upstairs, the congressman answered the phone and said send him up. The congressman's visitor, whoever that is, decides what a dandy time this would be to kill the son of a bitch. He does the deed, goes out, hides in the hallway, and waits for the contractor to walk into the trap. He might even exit the building and make the anonymous phone call to make damn *sure* the contractor gets caught in the trap. How does he get out? Same way he got in. I don't know specifically, but that's not my job. I can give you a theory or two. For one thing, maybe he lives in the building, which would account for no one seeing him go in. As for making the phone call, he could just go out and make it, because a tenant leaving his own building is not something anyone is going to notice or mention."

"That scenario has the killer making the phone call."

"Yes. For a specific reason. To trap the contractor."

"And why would the killer make the second phone call?"

"Same reason. To implicate the contractor. To complete the frame. So the cops will show up, find him hanging, think it was a murder-suicide."

She shook her head. "You're going around in circles. We already rejected the murder-suicide theory as making no sense."

"It makes no sense the way you tell it. But you may not have all the facts."

"Stop. Let's not go off on a tangent. Let's assume those phone calls weren't made by the killer *or* an innocent bystander. Let's assume those phone calls were made by a pain-in-the-ass, meddling PI who doesn't know any better than to leave well enough alone."

"What the hell would a PI be doing messing around is this case?"

"You tell me."

"I can't think of a reason."

"Neither can I. That's the big stumbling block here. If there were such a person, he would have to be a complete moron to get involved."

ADA Reynolds opened his mouth to say something.

She silenced him with a look. "Care to venture a guess how a PI might have gotten into the congressman's apartment?"

"Can't think of a thing. I can imagine a PI tailing the guy to his apartment, being unable to go in, and calling 911 in frustration to try to drive the guy out."

"You see that as a possible scenario?"

"Absolutely."

"Are you saying you did that?"

"Of course not."

"Why not?"

"It would be stupid as hell."

"I agree. Would you be willing to talk to the doorman of the building, see if you can work this out?"

"I asked to talk to the doorman. He said no."

"Things have changed. I think we can accommodate you." She pushed a button on the intercom. "Harold? See if you can get the doorman back in, will you?" she said and hung up.

"What's the point?" I asked.

She smiled. "You wanted to see the doorman. In the spirit of cooperation, I'm going to set it up. Put you two guys together and see what happens. You claim someone else could have gotten in. The doorman claims he couldn't. No reason not to let you guys duke it out."

"You expect me to get him to admit he's wrong?"

"I think you might trip him up. It will be fun to see you try."

The phone rang. She scooped it up, said, "Yes?" Listened, said thanks, and hung up. "Ten o'clock tomorrow morning. How's that sound."

"Great," I told her.

48

I was totally screwed. Next morning at ten o'clock the doorman would come walking into ADA Reynolds's office and identify me as the flower delivery man, and I could kiss my private eye license goodbye. And that was the best-case scenario. That was assuming I wasn't charged with murder and prosecuted for one homicide, if not two. At least then Richard would have to take an interest in the case. Still, it seemed a long way to go to attract his attention.

My only hope was to solve the case before then. The likelihood of which was approximately zero. It would be easier to kill the doorman. Now there was an idea. In this instance, it would probably be easier to get away with a crime I did commit than not commit it, and try to get away with the crimes I didn't. Unfortunately, I wasn't a killer. Which ruined my perfect scheme. My non-nefarious nature made it impossible for me to kill the doorman. Well, could I get someone *else* to kill the doorman? In all likelihood, it was possible. Not that I'd ever try such a thing. But if I bumbled around in my usual manner, given my track record there was a damn good chance it would actually happen.

I shook my head to clear it. Damn, I was getting punchy. Of course, standing on a precipice will do that. How the hell did I get out of it?

Okay.

It occurred to me that if the doorman wasn't available now, he was probably on duty. I could go over and see him. Talk to him prior to the meeting so the confrontation in front of the ADA wouldn't be such a shock. But what could I tell him? Come clean? That hardly seemed like a good idea. Invent some enormously complicated lie? That sounded better. Such as what? All right. How about some immensely complicated half truth? Now that seemed more likely. Admit to being a private eye, but deny everything else. Enlist his aid in fooling the ADA. Right. He'd be sure to go for that.

Except.

I knew he was lying about the phone call. If he blew the whistle on me, he'd be in the soup. I could point that out to him, suggest that he'd better play ball.

Good Lord. It occurred to me things had come to a pretty pass when blackmailing a material witness in a homicide case into giving perjured testimony looked like my best option.

My car, as if by its own accord, was wending its way through the 96th Street transverse to the East Side. That couldn't be good. The gods and the mechanical devices of the world were conspiring to push me into an ill-advised encounter. Should I talk to the doorman? Should I stop at the nearest newsstand and buy a lottery ticket? That probably had an equal chance of paying off.

Nonetheless, there I was, pulling up at a meter, and strolling around the block from Madison Avenue to survey the congressman's building from down the street.

I whipped my cell phone out of my pocket and called Alice. "Talk me out of it."

"What?"

"I'm thinking of having a heart-to-heart with the doorman."

"Don't do it."

"In an attempt to stave off a meeting tomorrow morning in front of the ADA."

"With the doorman?"

"Yeah."

"Don't do that either."

"How would you propose I avoid it?"

"Call Richard."

"Richard won't help me. Not for anything short of a murder."

"This is murder."

"I'm not charged with it."

"You will be if you meet the doorman."

I hung up and called Richard.

He wasn't pleased to hear from me.

I told him my predicament.

He was even less pleased. "You called up to have me talk you out of a suicidal line of action?"

"Didn't you hear what I said, Richard? Tomorrow morning it all blows up in my face."

"Call me when it does," Richard said, and hung up the phone.

I stood on the sidewalk, cursing Richard, cursing the doorman, cursing my fate.

The congressman's widow came out of the building. She was pushing a laundry cart. Filled with Gristedes bags. Full Gristedes bags. That didn't compute. People take laundry carts to the grocery store to bring bags of groceries home. No one takes bags of groceries back.

But that's what the widow was doing. And she was coming right at me. I ducked behind a parked car to let her go by.

I followed her three blocks up Fifth Avenue and into Central Park. It was a gorgeous afternoon, sunny and bright. It had probably been gorgeous all day, but I hadn't noticed. Easier to notice in the park. When you're not contemplating jail.

I followed at a discreet distance while the congressman's widow pushed the laundry cart along one of the paved walks to an athletic field where two soccer teams in uniform were practicing shots on their respective goals.

Which explained the laundry cart. The widow was a soccer mom and it was her turn to bring the snack. The bags would be full of cookies, oranges, and Gatorade.

Other parents had already gathered on the sidelines. As the widow bumped the cart along, the jock suddenly appeared out of the crowd to help her. She tried to wave him off, but he insisted. As he did, I had a revelation. Why was he there? He didn't have a son on the soccer team. So what was he doing there? Had he come just to meet the widow? That would seem horribly indiscreet, even for the most ardent of lovers. But that must be the case. Unless his wife was there. But why would she be?

I scoured the crowd for Mrs. Jock, and saw instead . . .

Sharon's mom!

I instinctively ducked out of sight. Had she seen me? Surely not, or she would have torn my head off. So, there she was, yet another grenade on life's grand grid of MineSweeper on which my territory was rapidly shrinking, where even a high school soccer game wasn't a safe place to be.

Then it occurred to me, what was she doing there? She didn't have a son on the team either.

The question immediately answered itself as the cheerleading squad, twelve boys and girls in purple in gold, ran onto the field, formed a circle, and broke apart into a choreographed little number. The girls looked happy to be there. The boys didn't. Or perhaps that's just my personal prejudice. I wouldn't have been happy to be there. I'd have wanted to be out on the field, kicking the ball. Even though I couldn't kick a soccer ball to save my life and wound up playing goalie, at least I played. Anyway, I shouldn't be an intolerant elitist jock snob. They also serve who only stand and cheer.

It was not until the end of the routine that I noticed one cheerleader stood out, though I couldn't be sure if that was true, or if I was merely prejudiced, since I knew her. But Sharon, the congressman's son's girlfriend, the falsely alleged teenage hooker and the source of all my troubles ever since the dawn of time, the star player, the featured cheerleader, the youngest, brightest, button-nosest, chirpiest cheerleader of them all, with lithe and limber moves, and a smile you could die for, was, at least for me, stealing the show.

It suddenly occurred to me that she was the key, she was the be-all and the end-all, that if only I could make it up with her, I could solve the whole thing, and it would all fall into place. I realized I was being duped by a TV catch phrase, from the first year of *Heroes*, "Save the cheerleader, save the world!" Which was my original premise, way back when. To save Sharon from a fate worse than death.

As if to punctuate my thoughts, the cheerleaders segued into an acrobatic sequence, with boys flipping girls, girls sliding though boys, legs in a cross-handed pull that must have been easy or the boys couldn't have handled it, but which looked amazingly hard, and wound up in a human pyramid. It was not that high, just six people, three, two, one, flanked and braced by the other six, but it was still impressive. At the pinnacle of the pyramid, smiling brightly from her perilous perch without the slightest trace of fear, was my nemesis, my undoing, my Achilles heel, the fair maiden I had mistakenly and ignominiously rescued.

At the base of the pyramid, peeking around one of the cornerstones, all but giggling in giddy fun, was Sharon's friend, who I'd seen practicing with her on the sidewalk, before my ill-fated Philadelphia trip.

Immediately my smile turned upside down, turned to a frown. Shit.

She accounted for the jock. He was here to see his daughter. Not for a clandestine rendezvous with a congressional widow. What I was witnessing was a high school soccer game and nothing more. It did not help me in any way except to pass the time. Which I did not want passed, as it continued to tick ever closer to my morning meeting with the doorman. And nothing could save me, because the jock wasn't hitting on the congressman's widow at all.

As if to punctuate the thought, Macho Man walked down the sideline and draped a large, muscular arm around the shoulders of his diminutive wife.

The congressman's widow was not glaring daggers at her. The congressman's widow was not paying the least bit of attention to either of them. The congressman's widow was gazing at the young man on the field who had stopped to watch the cheerleaders, the boy-band member staring with teenage ardor, smitten by the girl at the top of the pyramid.

49

"Suppose you were a competent detective."

"Alice."

Alice was looking good, in a simple cotton T-shirt and panties, standard nighttime gear. Alice seldom wore pajamas, unless it was really cold.

"I'm not trying to put you down. You are who you are. You're not your normal, everyday detective. But suppose you weren't Stanley Hastings, actor/writer, who fell into the PI shit as a job between gigs. Say you were just your average, regular detective. What could I expect?"

I looked at her, baffled. "Alice?"

"I come into your office, and you're a common, ordinary PI. Not some romantic fool influenced by movies, books, and TV."

"Is there a point to all this?"

"Absolutely. I come into your office and spin you a story that makes you feel sympathetic, and ask you to rescue my daughter from a life of sin. Now, what do I expect you to do?"

"Go out and rescue your daughter."

Alice made a face. "No. I expect you to fuck up. I've given you a load of information, a lot of it's bullshit, you're bound to fuck up and blow the whole thing sky-high. Do I ask you to dope her with chloral hydrate and bring her home? No. It never occurs to me that you might. My expectation of your being able to get her out of the nightclub and bring her home to New York is zero. I don't even expect you to try. I expect you to make a total hash of the situation that will result in someone calling the cops. That happened, but not until you managed to successfully abduct the girl. Which is something I hadn't foreseen. You weren't supposed to get arrested in New York. You were supposed to get arrested in the nightclub in Philadelphia. When you tried to get the girl away from the congressman, and she wouldn't go. Which would have happened if you were a competent detective, a normal detective, the type of detective the woman was trying to hire. Only I hired Stanley Hastings, white knight, who, against his own best interests, and at great personal risk, drugs the girl and drags her home. Wasn't supposed to happen. There was supposed to be a huge scene in the nightclub, resulting in cops, arrests, and the media gleefully reporting on the congressman being tailed by a New York private eye for sexual high jinks with the teenage girlfriend of his teenage son who was performing in a boy band. The press would have a field day. And all it took was your being a competent detective. No more, no less. See what I'm getting at?"

"You know you look lovely when you lecture?"

"So, you have to ask yourself. What if you were a competent detective? What if you were responsible for an ugly scene?"

"What if I were?"

"What would have happened then?"

"What are you getting at, Alice?"

"I was just thinking maybe you're going about this all wrong." She put up her hand. "I know, what a bizarre concept."

"Anytime you're through having fun."

"You assume someone was trying to embarrass the congressman. What if they weren't? What if the idea wasn't to embarrass the congressman? What if the idea was to embarrass the girl?"

"What?"

"Popular kid. Dating a singer in a boy band. Wouldn't you like to take her down a peg?"

"Sure, if I was one of her classmates. Then I wouldn't have the resources to do it. I mean, give me a break." I weighed them in my hands. "Teenage girl. Congressional figure. Who you gonna set up?"

"True. But who set them up?"

"What?"

"You never found your bogus mother."

"So?"

"How do you know *she* wasn't a teenage girl?"

"Oh, come on. You think I can't tell a girl from a woman?"

"What's the dividing line? Sixteen? Eighteen? Twenty-one? Thirty? How old was the phoney mother?"

"I don't know."

"You don't remember anything about her except she had a pair of tits. So she probably wasn't eight."

"That's unfair."

"Well, narrow it down for me. What are we talking here? Fifteen to forty-five?"

"That's in the ballpark."

"You're hopeless. So if the girl had bitchy classmates, jealous of her popularity . . ."

"She did."

"Oh?"

"Her best friend fits the profile. A lesser light, definitely second-string."

"So?"

"Scrawny little thing, gawky, undeveloped, probably hasn't gone through puberty."

"You think she's jealous?"

"I would be. She's just another cheerleader and her friend's the star."

"What's her mother like?"

"Her mother?"

"Yeah."

"Like her daughter. Mousy little nondescript woman. Why?"

"It's hard to get a clear picture when the reporter's so dull and vague." Alice frowned. "Something's not right."

"What?"

"Something you just told me. It doesn't add up."

"Of course it doesn't add up. The whole point is it doesn't add up."

"No. Something specific. Something bothered me. Now, what is it?" Alice snapped her fingers. "Got it! Why did you notice her?"

"What?"

"The mother. If the mother's so unattractive and nondescript, why would you notice her at all?"

"She was at the service."

"Huh?"

"She was at the memorial service. You saw her yourself."

"I did."

"Sure. She's married to the jock."

Alice gave me that pitying glance that always let me know I was being an idiot. She smiled and shook her head.

"Oh, Stanley."

50

I was nervous walking into ADA Reynolds's office. I didn't know what I was going to do. Alice had spun me a scenario of the case that I didn't buy for a minute, even with her in her slinky bedtime attire. Without her sitting there in a T-shirt and panties, Alice's theory lost all credibility whatsoever. Basically, I had nothing.

I tried to bluff it through. It didn't go well. Reynolds regarded me as if I were trying to sell him land on the moon.

"What the hell are you talking about?"

I didn't know. I was just talking. It was really little more than a filibuster to postpone the moment of truth when the doorman saw me and I was dead meat. I wanted to prepare ADA Reynolds for that moment. Not to mention his girlfriend, who was also there for the kill.

"All I'm saying is, if I feed the doorman a line of bullshit, just go with it. You know, in case you feel the urge to interrupt me, or arrest me, or jump over the table and strangle me. The type of things you're apt to do."

He squinted at me suspiciously. "Why are you babbling?"

"I'm afraid you'll do something you'll regret. If you ever wind up prosecuting this case, the guy's gonna be a witness. It would be better not to spill anything in front of him."

"Oh, thanks for the advice. I think I can handle it."

I finally ran out of stalls, and they brought the guy in. I braced myself for the inevitable.

The doorman gawked at me in surprise. "What are *you* doing here?"

ADA Reynolds frowned. "You know him?" he asked the doorman.

I beat the doorman to the punch. "He thinks he does." I smiled at him. "Bad news, friend. I'm here to prove you're lying."

The doorman scowled. "What?"

"Wait a minute." ADA Reynolds cut me off, said to the doorman. "You know this man?"

"That's the flower delivery guy."

"What?!"

I shot ADA Reynolds a look. "He thinks I'm the flower delivery guy. Only one of the many things he got wrong. Wanna hear the others?"

"I wanna hear about *this*. Why do you think he's the flower delivery guy?"

"He delivered flowers. To Mrs. Finnegan. She *liked* him."

"Did she say that, or did I?"

The doorman looked utterly baffled. Of course, ADA Reynolds didn't look much better. He was about to jump back in, so I forged ahead.

"Which totally disproves your testimony. You claim no one could get in. I got in with no more ID than a bunch of flowers.

But you don't know where I went after I got upstairs. I could have gone anywhere. Including the congressman's apartment. So, when you testify with such solemn conviction that no one called on the congressman, the truth is, you don't know."

The ADA blinked twice. "Is that true?"

He was talking to me, but I turned it on the doorman. "How about it? Is that true?"

The doorman gawked at me. "Who the hell are you?"

"I'm a private eye working for Hanson's lawyer to undercut your story. Unfortunately, he's dead, and can't profit from it, but that doesn't affect the significance of my work."

"Wait a minute," ADA Reynolds said. "*When* did you deliver those flowers?"

"I delivered them when *he* was on duty. He was on duty, I showed him the flowers and gave him the apartment number of a woman who lived in the building. I went upstairs, hung out for a half hour, and came back down."

The doorman was beside himself. "You said she invited you in. For a matinee! You joked you about it."

"And you believed it. Which proves my point. You're a credulous fool, and the killer would have no problem putting one over on you." I smiled at ADA Reynolds. "Which is good news for you, if you want to prosecute someone else for killing the congressman. I mean, it's hard to prosecute a dead man."

ADA Reynolds was livid. All my admonitions about not jumping in went right out the window. Except for one. Spilling stuff in front of the guy. Reynolds jerked his thumb at the doorman, barked, "Take him outside."

ADA Fairfield arched her eyebrows. "*Excuse* me?"

He flushed, strode to the door, motioned to a court officer. "Watch him." He pushed the doorman out, slammed the door, and turned back on me. "All right. Talk."

I shrugged. "You know the back story. I was set up to frame the congressman, it didn't happen, I wasn't satisfied, wouldn't drop it, nosed around."

"Are you saying you called on the congressman disguised as a flower delivery man?"

"I am specifically *not* saying that. And I would be particularly unhappy if I was misquoted as *having* said that."

"You admit you got into the building by tricking the doorman."

"Admit? There's an inflammatory word with legal ramifications. Are you telling me I need counsel?"

"You're going to need a doctor if you don't stop horsing around."

"Honey," ADA Fairfield warned.

Talk about loaded words. On that one dangled the fate of the entire relationship up to and including ADA Reynolds's chance of getting lucky anytime in the near future.

He controlled himself with an effort. "No one's accusing anyone of anything. But I'd like to know what the hell is going on."

"Me too," I said. "Let's get the doorman back in here and find out."

It almost worked.

"No so fast," he said. "There's some questions I want answered. *When* did you scam the doorman? Was if before or after the murder?"

"After."

"Are you sure?"

"Absolutely."

"So you didn't see the congressman?"

"I saw him at the memorial service."

"You didn't see him alive?"

"No, I didn't."

"Then why did you go to his apartment?"

"I'm not saying I went to his apartment. I'm saying I went upstairs in the building, and I *could* have gone to his apartment."

ADA Fairfield stepped in again. "Mr. Hastings, why did you come here?"

"You called me in. To meet the doorman."

"That's not what I mean, and you know it. Why did you come to us in the first place?"

"I wasn't satisfied Leslie Hanson was guilty. It occurred to me the doorman could be lying or mistaken." I jerked my thumb at ADA Reynolds. "I tried to advance that theory to him, and he told me to take a hike. I tested my theory on the doorman, and damned if it wasn't right."

"So you called Hanson's lawyer?" ADA Reynolds said, accusingly.

"I didn't say that."

"Yes, you *did*. You said he *hired* you."

"That's what I told the *doorman*. It was bullshit. I was bluffing. Hanson's lawyer never hired me."

"So you say."

ADA Fairfield put up her hand. "Let's not get sidetracked. Never mind if anyone hired you. The fact is, you managed get into the building without proper authorization."

"Would that be a crime?"

"Delivering flowers? I'd have to look at the penal code."

ADA Reynolds scowled. "Oh, for Christ's sake. Can we get on with it?"

She smiled. "I'm sorry."

He flushed. "Not you."

I seized the opportunity to divert the conversation. "But that's only one of the ways the killer could have gotten in."

"You have others?" ADA Fairfield said. "Like what?"

"Bring the doorman back in. Let me ask him a couple of questions."

"Ask him what?" ADA Reynolds demanded.

"If anyone could have gotten by him."

"Oh, right. Like he's gonna say yes."

"I'll phrase it differently. Come on. What have you got to lose?"

ADA Reynolds wasn't sold, but his girlfriend tipped the scale. The doorman was marched back in.

"Okay," I said. "Now, from the time the congressman got home to the time he got killed, to the best of your knowledge—and I say to the best of you knowledge because we have already demonstrated that your knowledge is none too good—the only one who called on him was Leslie Hanson. Is that right?"

"Yes." The doorman said it through clenched teeth.

"And how do you know what time the congressman got home?"

"I saw him."

"Did you speak to him?"

"He didn't come through the lobby. He came in the garage."

"How'd you see him in the garage?"

"On the video monitor."

"Really? You saw his car drive in?"

"That's right."

"How do you know the congressman was driving it?"

"I saw his face. Plain as day. If you don't believe me, see for yourself."

"The camera is angled so you can see the driver driving in?"

"That's right."

"Then you must *not* be able to see his face when he goes out."

"So?"

"Is that true? You couldn't see his face driving out?"

"He didn't drive out. He came home and he got killed."

"Stick with me here. If he *had* driven out, you wouldn't have seen his face, because on the way *out*, the camera is pointing at the *passenger's* side window."

"Yes."

"And you can't see who's in the *driver's* side window when the car is going *out*."

"No, I can't. So what?"

"So you can't see who's in the *passenger's* side window driving *in.*"

The doorman frowned.

ADA Reynolds's eyes widened. "Son of a bitch!"

I smiled at him. "Care to watch some video?"

51

IT WAS UNPRODUCTIVE. EXCEPT TO CONFIRM MY HYPOTHESIS. As the congressman drove in, you could see his face, but you could not see far enough into the car to know if he had a passenger aboard. Which blew the doorman's testimony out of the water, any bogus flower deliveries notwithstanding.

"So," I said. "Looks like we gotta watch the rest of it."

ADA Reynolds frowned. "What for?"

"See if anyone suspicious went out through the garage."

"How would we know they were suspicious?"

"Well, anyone he didn't recognize."

"But you can't see the drivers going out of the garage."

"Well, any *car* he didn't recognize."

The doorman shook his head. "Unauthorized cars can't get in."

"Right," I said. "Just like unauthorized people."

"They don't have a zapper. They can't open the door."

"And no one could steal a zapper," I said. "It's a crime. Of course, so is murder."

"You can see the drivers' faces going in. No one's letting in a strange car with a strange driver."

"Of course not," I said. "The system's infallible. Never mind. How about having him look for someone he knew."

"Like who?"

"I don't know. Like the congressman's wife? Surely he'd have recognized her."

"Surely he'd have mentioned it."

"Would he? Why would he even notice? He didn't know there was going to be a murder. I'm sure keeping track of the tenants' comings and goings is not a high priority."

"I'd have noticed," the doorman said angrily.

"How about someone on foot?" I said. "Let's see if there's anyone walking out."

"No one goes out through the garage."

"They might if they just killed a congressman. That garage door open from the inside? Or would the killer have to wait until a car drove in to slip out before the door closed? Whoever came in the congressman's car sure didn't leave in it. They'd have to find another way to go."

We watched the video. It was unrewarding. No one on foot, no cars the doorman didn't know.

"Are you satisfied?" he said. "Can I go now?"

"Yes," I said.

Just a little too quickly.

Damn.

I'd been so careful, played it so well. And then, inches from victory, I pull a bonehead mistake like that.

"Hold on," ADA Reynolds said, and I knew I was in the soup. He spoke to the doorman, but looked at me. "You're not going anywhere until you tell me what this guy doesn't want you to." He pointed his finger in my face. "Now you shut up and I'll ask the questions. And you, look at me. Don't look at him. I'm suddenly more interested in this guy's visit to your building. What can you tell me about that?"

"Well, actually, he came twice."

Shit.

"Twice? Are you sure?"

"Sure. Because the second time he was asking me all about the murder."

"What?"

"Yeah. I told him about the murder, and he decided not to go up."

"You told him about the murder?"

"Yes."

"The second time he came to the building?"

"Right."

"Why didn't you tell him about the murder the first time he came to the building?"

The doorman frowned. "I guess it hadn't happened yet."

52

"OKAY, I ADMIT IT LOOKS BAD."

"Looks bad? It doesn't just *look* bad. You're one step away from needing an attorney. I can't wait to hear your explanation. It seems to me there are two possibilities. Either you killed the congressman, or . . ." He paused, frowned, considered. "Maybe there's only *one* possibility."

"Then you haven't been paying attention. Studying the videotape was not just an exercise in misdirection. It's a legitimate way the murderer could have gotten in and out."

"I don't care how many ways the murderer could have gotten in. The fact is, you *did*. Now, you want to tell me about it?"

I certainly didn't. The doorman, under a grueling interrogation, to which I was not privy, had either remembered, or been led to believe he remembered, that my visit to his building had happened on the very day the congressman was killed. Odds were he was probably pretty clear on the point, because I seemed

234

to remember discussing that very fact with him during that second visit.

Making matters worse was the fact that I had no idea what the doorman had actually said, so discussing it was like walking through a minefield. All in all, I was royally screwed.

"Care to explain what you were doing in the congressman's apartment building on the day of the murder *before* the murder?"

"See, this is why I need a lawyer. If my lawyer were here, I'm sure he would point out that question assumes facts not in evidence. How do you know I went there before the murder? Have you established the time of the murder? If so, *I* wasn't notified, and I bet the doorman wasn't either. If he says I was there before the murder, I would like to know how the hell he knows."

ADA Reynolds started to get up, but his girlfriend pulled him back down.

"I don't think you understand what's happening here," she said. "You want to spout legal mumbo jumbo, you're only making it harder on yourself."

I was grateful for her help, but not that grateful. "That's nice of you. But I'm not splitting hairs. Whether I went there before or after the murder is hardly a minor point."

"The why don't you clear it up for us?"

"There's nothing to clear up. I went there after the murder. That's what I said then, and that's what I say now. I don't care what your witness says. I've already demonstrated what his testimony is worth."

"You've shown he might be mistaken. There's no indication he was lying."

"Then he might be mistaken about me."

"But he's not. As far as he's concerned, you went in there before the murder. I don't know if that's true, but the fact is he believes it. Which establishes on thing. You went in before *he* knew there was a murder. In other words, before the cops arrived and arrested

Mr. Hanson. You were there before Mr. Hanson. Would you care to explain how that happened?"

"Not really."

"I wasn't offering you an option."

"You gonna insist on an answer?"

"Yes, I am."

"To bad. That will involve a formal charge, a Miranda warning, and lawyers. Just when we were doing so well."

ADA Fairfield was getting exasperated too. "Damn it. We're trying to give you a break."

If they were, I wouldn't have known it. I was fucked, and fucked bad. It was time to give Alice's theory a try. Not that I believed in it for a moment, but I didn't have anything else.

I took a breath. "You wanna give me a break? Let's make a deal."

ADA Reynolds smelled a rat. "Deal? What deal?"

"I still think the doorman's off base. I'll answer questions about the time I went upstairs posing as a flower delivery man, if the doorman can substantiate his claim."

"Substantiate it how?"

"Pick me out of a lineup."

Reynolds gawked. "A lineup?"

"Yeah. A police lineup. But not with usual clerks and detectives you throw together. I'd like the congressman's widow. I'd like the jock and his wife. I'd like Mr. and Mrs. Weldon."

"Who?"

"That's more in her ballpark. The parents of the congressman's son's girlfriend."

"Are you serious?"

"Absolutely."

"You think he can't pick you out of that lineup."

"I'd like to see him try."

53

IT WAS A ZOO.

The widow was understandably upset. Sharon's parents were irate, but then, they hated me anyway. And the jock and his wife seemed confused. None of them had any idea what was going on. Since I was the only one who did, I had to explain.

"It's very simple." I addressed the widow. "The doorman of your building has identified me as going up to your apartment the day your husband was killed. I dispute his version of the events, and I've challenged him to pick me out of a lineup. You're the lineup."

"You're out of your mind," Sharon's father said. "We don't have to put up with this."

"No, you don't. But if you refuse, your refusal becomes a matter of record. And then the police will take an interest in you when they find they have nowhere else to go."

He turned angrily on the attractive ADA. "You said we were finished with this."

"That was before there was a murder. Obviously, things are different now."

"Not to us. We have nothing to do with it. Why are we here?"

"He asked for you."

"And he gets whatever he wants?"

ADA Fairfield smiled, placatingly. She had a nice smile. "He's become a suspect in a murder. We tend to humor suspects, on the theory if you give them enough rope, they'll hang themselves."

It was a good argument. Not that it satisfied him, but at least it shut him up.

With only moderate bitching and moaning, the six of us were herded down the hall to the shadow box. It was your typical lineup box, long and narrow, with one-way glass in front, and a white wall with black height marks in back.

"All right," ADA Reynolds said. "If you've never been in a lineup before, I'm sure you've seen one on TV. You go in, stand on the number I give you, face the mirror. When I tell you to, step forward. If I ask you to speak, repeat what I tell you to say." He surveyed the group. "Okay, wise guy. You got five spaces, and six people. How you wanna handle that?"

The jock's wife begged off. She tended to defer to her husband, was probably used to being excluded.

"We're not so formal," I said. "Stand with your husband. We'll make room."

The jock wasn't going to hear it from me. He put his arm around his wife protectively, looked to ADA Reynolds for confirmation.

"Yeah, whatever," ADA Reynolds said. "Okay, take the positions I give you."

He put Sharon's father on space one, his wife on space two, me on space three, the jock and his wife on space four, and the congressman's widow on space five.

"Okay. We're going out front. Just stay on your spot until I call you on the microphone."

He and ADA Fairfield left us there. Everyone was glaring at me. I had a feeling if nothing happened soon, they would tear me to shreds.

The light came on and the microphone crackled.

"Can you hear me?" ADA Reynolds said. "All right, when I call your number, take one step forward."

We could hear the voice of the doorman in the background. "Why? It's the one in the middle."

"Are you sure?"

"This is stupid. Of course it's the one in the middle."

"It's *always* the one in the middle," I said. "The guy's not identifying a person, he's identifying a number. Turn out the lights, let me mix 'em up, and we'll do it again."

"I don't think so."

"Why not? You afraid he can't do it?"

"Of course he can do it."

"I bet he can't. Turn out the lights, we'll put the people where *I* want 'em, and see what he says then."

It was hard getting him to go along, considering how stupid it actually was, but he finally gave in with the air of an indulgent parent humoring a stubborn child.

"All right," I said, "let's mix 'em up. First off, I'm out of the middle. So who shall we put there? How about you?" I said to the jock.

He stuck his chin out at me. "Why?"

"Someone has to. Let's put your wife on one side. Here, you be number two." I pointed to Sharon's mother. "And we'll put *his* wife on the other side. You be number four, Mrs. Weldon. Now, then, I don't want to be number one." I pointed at Sharon's father. "So that's you. Then I'm number five." I made a face. "That's no good either." I pointed to the jock's wife. "You, change places with me. Now I'm number two, and you're number five. Perfect."

I looked the lineup over, feigned surprise. "Now there's no room for the congressman's wife. How about right in the middle with you?" I said to the jock. "I'm sure your wife won't mind."

The voice of ADA Reynolds crackled over the speaker. "How you coming in there?"

"Almost ready. Everyone all set? No, we're not. Mrs. Blake, if you would please stand in the middle."

The congressman's widow reluctantly joined the jock on number three.

"Okay," I said.

The lights came on.

The voice of the doorman said, "Number two."

I made a face. "Did anyone ask you? This guy's jumping the gun. He's answering before he's asked."

The doorman was totally exasperated. "What *possible* difference could *that* make?"

"More than you think," I said. "Now, before you say anything else, would you let me do this my way, or do we have to mix 'em up and start again?"

"Oh, for God's sakes!"

"Hang on," ADA Reynolds said to the doorman. To me he said, "What do you want?"

I couldn't see him, but I could tell he was talking through clenched teeth.

"I want people to step forward when told to. I want them to repeat simple phrases when asked."

"What do you want them to say?"

"I'll tell them as we go along. I'll tell them to step forward, and I'll tell them what to say."

"And this will confuse me into not being able to identify you?" the doorman said, sarcastically.

"Hang on," I told him. "You'll get your chance. Now then, if we may proceed. Number five. Please step forward."

The jock's wife stepped forward.

"Good. Step back. Number one. Step forward."

Sharon's father glared at me, but he stepped forward.

"Good. Step back. Number four. Step forward."

Sharon's mother stepped forward.

"Good. Step back. Number three, step forward."

The jock and the congressman's wife looked at each other.

"Good," I said. "Hold that pose."

They didn't, of course. They both turned to glare at me.

"What do you think you're doing?" the congressman's widow demanded.

"It's an experiment. Now, they didn't hold the pose, but tell me this. Did you ever see these two look at each other in the way they did just now?"

The jock scowled. "Hey, what the hell is this?"

The widow said," How dare you!"

"All right, Mr. Hastings," ADA Reynolds said. "That's enough."

"How about it?" I persisted. "Ever see them?"

"I . . . I can't remember," the doorman said.

"Interesting. He doesn't say yes, he doesn't say no. He says he can't recall. I like that. Okay, you two step back. Oh, you didn't step forward. Never mind." I turned to the jock's wife. "Number five, step forward."

I didn't wait for her to comply, but went right on. "Now look at number three and say, 'Get away from my husband, you bitch!'"

Her nostrils flared, her eyes blazed. "The hell I will!"

I pointed at her. "There! Did you see that? Look at her and tell me if this is the woman you saw going out through the lobby on the day of the murder."

The jock wheeled on me. "You son of a bitch!"

"Don't be stupid," I told him. "Look at your wife."

He turned, looked.

Her mouth was trembling, but no sound was coming out.

In the silence that followed, the doorman's puzzled voice came crackling over the microphone.

"You know, I think I *did* see her going out."

54

SHE CAVED.

It didn't take much. The doorman's ID freaked her out. Which wasn't much of an ID. Hardly any, when you came right down to it. Any good defense attorney could rip it to shreds. But his simple, sincere "I think I did see her," had a chilling effect on the woman, and if her husband hadn't stepped in to hold her up, I think she might have collapsed. The jock was, to all intents and purposes, a good husband, who wasn't having an affair with the congressman's wife. They were just good friends, the two families, better friends than the jerky Weldons whose daughter the congressman's son was seeing. It was too bad his son didn't like their daughter. But that wasn't going to happen, at least not then, with the gawky caterpillar as yet unraised to butterfly status. Not that it was a huge problem, the one daughter more popular than the other, the one with the boyfriend, star of the cheerleading team, much like the TV movie about the murdering cheerleader mother, if there really was such a thing. I only remember it vaguely.

That was the key.

The jock's wife was having an affair with the congressman. Which was fine, while they were just two big, happy families. But after the congressman became congressman, and decided to cool it with the jock's wife, before he became the butt of every standup monologue, things went straight downhill. His son picking Sharon and passing up their darling daughter was the last straw. The jock's wife snapped with the fury of woman twice scorned, as a lover and as a mother.

The jock's wife swore to get even.

And here I have to apologize for my entire sex, having been totally duped by a wig and a Victoria's Secret Miracle Bra. If you think that can't happen, I didn't either. I looked right at the woman, and I didn't know. She presented without tits, hair, and makeup, as a plain woman of no particular notice. Feel free here to hang me up by my sexist scrotum. But I remember when I was kid a ten-year-old girl I met in camp about as pretty as your average sack of potatoes turned up in high school—va va voom!—an absolute knockout driving all the guys crazy.

Just like the jock's wife. A little war paint, fake hair, and her tits pushed up to the limit, and I didn't have a clue. It worked on me, and her setup should have worked on the congressman. After all, I was perfectly programmed to blow the whole deal. There was no way I was getting the girl away from him without making a scene. No way the story didn't wind up on the local if not the national news. So embarrassing for him, so embarrassing for her, two birds with one stone.

Ah, but she figured without the white knight on the steed, rescuing the damsel in distress. Granted, my chance of succeeding was a long shot. Still, it should have been *no* shot. No PI in his right mind would have attempted what I did. But I countered her caper, foiled her nefarious scheme, and sent her back to the drawing board, angry, enraged, ready to take things into her own hands.

So, she calls the congressman, tries a little good old-fashioned extortion. *You don't want to see me anymore, fine, I'll go to the papers.* He pleads with her to reconsider, she agrees to talk it over. He picks her up in his car, drives her to his building. Pulls into the garage, just as they used to do. With her in the passenger seat, the doorman won't see.

They go upstairs. She pours out her heart. She wants him back.

She swears she never meant to kill him. She threw herself at him. He pushed her away. Assaulted her. She was defending herself when she picked up the andiron. So she says, and so her lawyer will undoubtedly plead. Whether a jury will buy it or not is another matter. At any rate, she is suddenly faced with the unpleasant realization that the congressman is dead. She pulls herself together and gets the hell out of there.

She does it by walking right through the lobby. It's no big deal. She's done it before. She figures the doorman won't notice. She figures right. The guy's job is to screen people going into the building, not to monitor people going out. In the normal course of events, there's no reason for him to notice her. Even once the murder is discovered, the police are only concerned with who went in. If not for my little stunt, the guy might not have remembered her at all. His identification, tentative as it was, and coming so late, was shaky at best. A good defense attorney could have ripped him to shreds.

If she hadn't confessed.

Which left self-defense. Self-defense was the icing on the cake. It was hard to argue with that. It might well have been self-defense.

But not Leslie Hanson. That was another story altogether. If I were a prosecutor, that's the case I would pick. There's only one way that plays out. And I hate it like hell, because it comes back to me. And it's going to be awhile before I can forgive myself. Because I told Hanson's attorney. And Hanson's attorney told Hanson. And Hanson went looking for the jock. Only the jock was in Cleveland. So Hanson didn't find the jock. He found the jock's wife.

He told her what he knew. He was wrong, of course, like I was, but it was close enough to scare the living daylights out of her. So she strung him along. Fed him some bullshit story, got him to take her back to his apartment. The same way she got me to follow the girl, by using sex and charm, and reminding me constantly that she had the necessary working-girl parts to fulfill my adolescent dreams. Her husband was innocent, but she couldn't stand to see him unfairly smeared. He had no alibi, might even be convicted, and she'd do anything to see that wouldn't happen.

The anything in question was the type that would require retiring to his apartment.

His show of good faith was to write, not a promise not to accuse her husband—that would be worthless, he could go back on his word at any time with no consequences to him whatsoever—but an apology to the widow for causing a scene at her memorial service, saying it was entirely his fault, and the guy who tackled him was not to blame, the theory being that having written such a letter, it would be hard to subsequently accuse the guy of the murder.

I'm not sure that made total sense, but give a guy a chance to get laid, and total sense is not necessarily a prerequisite. Hanson went for it. She went back to his apartment, sat him down, and dictated a letter to the congressman's widow. At her direction, he wrote: *I'm sorry I interrupted your memorial service.*

Or, he would have, if she hadn't coshed a sap down on the back of his head right after he wrote the word *sorry*, creating the impression he was writing a suicide note, beginning: *I'm sorry I killed your husband. I can't live with myself anymore,* et cetera, et cetera. Which the police bought, hook, line, and sinker.

She dragged him into the bathroom, tied a rope around his neck, threw it over the shower rod, and hauled him up. She tied it off to the faucet, brought a straight chair into the bathroom, and maneuvered him up on it. Tightened and retied the rope so he was standing on his tiptoes.

And then took the chair away.

His feet dangled down just shy of the bathroom floor, hanging him by the neck until dead.

She removed the chair from the bathroom, and placed the note underneath the dangling body, giving credulous fools the impression that the gentleman had written a suicide note, climbed on the edge the tub, and hung himself in a fit of remorse.

All of this, she insisted, was done without the help of her husband, who really was in Cleveland, and whom she really loved, her dalliance with the congressman not withstanding.

She confessed, in large part, for the purpose of saving him.

Her confession satisfied the police. It didn't satisfy me. Oh, I believed it, it was just rather unsatisfactory, as far as I was concerned, that the attractive young damsel in distress who had come to me for help would wind up convicted of murder. It was not the feel-good outcome I had hoped for. Add in my guilt over Leslie Hanson, and I wasn't exactly dancing on the clouds.

The kicker was, I hadn't even figured it out myself. I didn't have that *aha!* moment of clarity where everything comes together. It had taken Alice making the leap of logic to the Texas Cheerleader Murdering Mom, or whatever the hell that was, that turned out to be at least partially true. So the credit was really hers. Not that I begrudge it to her.

He said, diplomatically.

Of course, I took it from there. That's what I could feel good about. The fact that, armed with Alice's deductions, I had walked into the ADA's office and bluffed myself, alone, unaided, and without benefit of attorney, through one of the most extraordinary witness identification sequences in the history of law enforcement. I had maneuvered the witness who identified me as the man he had seen at the scene of the crime on the day of the murder into identifying a woman instead.

All right, *instead* is a bit of stretch, he identified me first, and only identified her as an afterthought. Still, it worked. I had begun as the most likely suspect. *The man who will be suspected of murder upon walking into the ADA's office is most likely to be* . . . See? It just doesn't work. I can't think of a name that fits.

Nonetheless, I had turned it on its ear. Bluffed the ADA, buffaloed him to a standstill, forced him to give me the lineup I wanted, and exposed the real killer. So, in the greater scheme of things, when I look at the spectacular mess I had made of the case, there was at least one tiny ray of light.

55

"So, you got everything straightened out?" Richard said.

"That's right."

"And you did it without dragging me into it."

"I thought you liked murder cases."

"I murder *trials*," Richard said. "Murder cases in *court*. This one never got there. It was merely a murder *investigation*. Which are no fun at all."

"I'm sorry you feel that way."

"Well, how do you expect me to feel? I'm a trial lawyer. Court is exciting, flashy, fun. The rest is just work."

"I'm sorry you didn't get to defend me in front of a jury."

"I'm not. A simple, boring case. Hardly worth the time."

"I'm sorry if I bored you with it."

"Not at all. I don't mind *hearing* about the case. I just didn't want to *do* anything. So the woman confessed. How'd you manage that?"

I told him about the shadowbox lineup.

"And they let you get away with it?"

"Just barely."

"But they did?"

"Yeah."

"How come?"

"They wanted to get something on me. Once the doorman identified me as going into the building, that bumped me up to prime suspect. They were willing to let me do anything that might end up having me hang myself."

"Even so. Taking over the lineup. Telling the witnesses what to do. I'm surprised ADA Reynolds went for it."

"He wasn't thrilled. Actually, ADA Fairfield talked him into it."

"Oh? She was there?"

"Yeah."

"And she took your side? Went to bat for you?"

"Actually, she did."

"And that made a difference?"

"Yeah. I think ADA Reynolds would have crucified me."

"But he listened to her?"

"Yeah, he did." I exhaled, bit the bullet. "Richard?"

"Yeah."

"You seem rather fond of ADA Fairfield. So I think you ought to know. The reason he listened to her is he's her boyfriend."

Richard raised his eyebrows. "Actually, they're engaged."

I stared at him. "You knew that?"

"Well, of course. I'm not the type of lawyer to proceed without precedent. When I noticed how attractive this ADA was, I asked around. Found out she was going with another ADA right here in Manhattan. It was a stroke of luck when he got assigned to the congressman killing, what with you taking such an interest in it. When it looked like you were in trouble, I took her out to dinner, explained the situation, and enlisted her help. She did a number on her boyfriend?"

"She sure did."

"Well, she better. That was an expensive dinner. Not that I begrudge you, you understand. I do have to eat, and dining with an attractive ADA was far more pleasant than bailing you out of whatever scrape you got in."

So. The crowning blow. Alice was right again, even when she was just kidding, making jokes about billable hours, and Richard dating an ADA to do me a good turn. Alice was right, and I was a schmuck, thinking I'd done it all by myself like a big boy, not realizing I'd had training wheels on my bike.

I started laughing uncontrollably. I couldn't stop myself.

Richard stared at me. "Stanley? What is it?"

I waved my hand at him, the way you will when you're laughing too hard to speak, and someone's waiting for a response.

"What's so funny?"

"What you said should decimate me, but it makes my day. It puts everything in perspective. I get by with a little from my friends. Nothing wrong with that."

He smiled, not understanding.

I couldn't explain it to Richard. I couldn't explain it to myself. I couldn't explain it to Alice, though she could probably explain it to me. But finding out I had a guardian angel guiding me through was just too darn funny.

Not that it made everything all right. Far from it. I still blamed myself for Leslie Hanson's murder. It would be a long time before I got over that. I probably never will.

But at least I could still laugh at my own foibles.

I don't know if that's good or bad.